Raul Castenada is a born loser — at fifteen, he has been hurt so many times that he has lost all touch with his emotions, and will go along with almost anything an older boy does.

Razor Daniels, on the other hand, plays the game to win. A black, twenty-four-year-old stick-up artist, he enjoys the fear he elicits in rich whiteys, as he wages his one-man war against them.

Keith Lawson is the personification of all that Daniels hates. At seventeen, he has everything money can buy — and an alcohol problem that is about to ruin what's left of his life.

Hell·Bound

Hell·Bound

Don Wilkerson
with David Manuel

PARACLETE PRESS
Orleans, MA 02653

Copyright © 1978 by Don Wilkerson and David Manuel
ISBN: 0–941478–41–6
Library of Congress Catalog Card Number: 78-60735
All Rights Reserved
Published by Paraclete Press
Orleans, MA 02653
Printed in the United States of America

Preface

Don Wilkerson and I sat in the living room of his home at Camp Champion, tucked into the wooded foothills of New York's Catskill Mountains.

"What I really want to do," Don was saying, "is capture the spirit of what happens at Teen Challenge. When you wrote *The Jesus Factor,* you did that for the Farm, all right, but it was still an outsider, looking in. I want to get inside, somehow . . . show what happens inside a guy going through the program and what makes him want to change."

Don's wife Cindy brought us each a Tab, and I was grateful for the interruption, because we had been through all of this before. "The only way to do that," I said again, "is to follow two or three guys through. Only to make it believable, we're going to have to tell everything, including exactly what they were into before, and what they came out of, and that's usually the bottom of the barrel. But you've got to do it, or it won't wash."

He shook his head. "We can't do that. We're not going to prejudice any graduate's new life in Christ that way. Who do you think is going to hire a kid who has twenty-one counts of arson against him? Do you think they're going to care how deeply committed to the Lord his life is now?" He fell silent, and I had nothing more to say. I was supposed to leave the next day with a

5

completed outline, and we hadn't even started.

And then, all of a sudden, I had it: "Composites. We'll take three characters, base them on real people and real incidents, but draw from so many case histories and backgrounds and traits, that when we're done, we'll have created three original personalities. If we do it right, only the guy who was actually involved in a given incident will be able to recognize himself. Then if he wants to identify himself, that's his business."

"And that way," said Don, warming to the idea, "we'll be able to get inside them and see why they did what they did — perhaps even more so than if we were dealing with actual testimonies."

I nodded. "We'll also be able to let things happen that actually do happen, only never really get told, like the conflicts that come up between the guys. And we'll have the freedom to concentrate on the crucial moments and condense the rest."

And so we began, Don providing the expertise, and the two of us working out plot line. *Raul Castenada,* I wrote at the top of my note pad, as Don sketched in his background. *Fifteen years of age. Lives in the south Bronx with his mother, who's the head of the house. Has a "weekend father" who works at the post office [explain weekend father], and an older brother on Methadone maintenance. Raul sniffs glue . . . .*

David Manuel

6

To
the Teen Challenge staff and workers,
past and present,
who have given so unstintingly of themselves,
and whose work and witness for Christ
has affected the lives of so many —
this book is gratefully dedicated.

1

The Glue-sniffer

A muffled giggle broke the silence. In the gloom of the gathering January dusk, three shadows passed by a broken window, finding their way into the darkest recesses of the condemned tenement building. There was the sound of fumbling, a half-uttered curse, and then a match flared, illuminating three faces — young faces, their brows furrowed in concentration. Two of the boys, intent on fishing out and lighting up home-rolled cigarettes, were perhaps sixteen or seventeen; the third, holding a brown paper bag with something wet in the bottom, was slightly younger.

"Ow!" said the boy holding the match, as it burned down to his fingers. He dropped it, and all three of them laughed as the darkness enveloped them, no longer cautious of how far their voices might carry.

"Light another, man!" commanded the oldest. "I haven't got this joint going yet. Man, it's cold in here!"

Another match burst into flame, and the oldest boy grabbed the hand that held it and brought it close enough to light the ragged cigarette between his lips. He inhaled as deeply as he could, filling all the space in his chest and holding it as long as possible before exhaling.

The boy holding the match, anxious to gain the leader's favor, now held the match lower and said, "Hey, Eddie, did you catch the new shoes my man here has on?" And he indicated the feet of the younger boy.

Taking another drag, composed of rapid little inhales, Eddie stooped to examine them. "Oh, yeah!" he said slowly in appreciation, and the younger boy started to smile. "What!" Eddie said, his tone suddenly cutting, "did they fall off a Salvation Army truck?" And he and the other boy went into gales of laughter, as darkness again descended. "People like you, Lightnin', shouldn't try to dress cool; it's worse than if you didn't try at all." And again the other two laughed.

There was silence for a moment, save for the sound of several puffs in quick succession and the rattling of the paper bag being breathed into.

"Hey, Lightnin'," said Eddie, "how come you won't turn on with Chico and me? We'll give you the grass."

" 'Cause I like sniffing glue," the younger boy replied.

"But that's kid stuff! You're fifteen years old!" He waited for a reply, but there was none. The end of the joint glowed in the darkness. "Light another match," Eddie said to Chico. "I

10

want to see what's turning this young man on."

Chico did as directed, and Eddie snatched the bag away from the younger boy and peered into it. He took a sniff and wrinkled his nose, snorting in dusgust. "Man, that stuff's *awful*. It'll rot your brain, for sure!" Just then, the match burned down, and Chico dropped it into the bag that Eddie held, which caught fire. The younger boy reached for the bag to try to save it, but Eddie held him at bay, holding the bag until it was half consumed and then flinging it away, onto a pile of trash in a corner. "Leave it alone," he said to the younger boy. "You're better off without it. Now, come on; it just so happens I got an extra joint stashed away in the next room." And he and Chico led the way, followed reluctantly by the younger boy.

Eddie had just retrieved the fresh joint and was lighting it from the burning end of the one he had been smoking, when Chico said, "Hey!" and pointed towards the doorway they had just come through. Shadows were leaping and dancing in a dull orange pantomime, and they hurried back to the doorway. The trash pile on which Eddie had flung the burning paper bag was now itself ablaze. The younger boy rushed in to try to put it out, but it was already beyond what they could cope with, flames licking up the tinder dry walls. "Come on!" shouted Eddie. "Ain't no way we're gonna put that out! Let's get the hell outa here!" And he bolted for the outside doorway, Chico and the younger boy following him.

Emerging into the night, the three figures were silhouetted for a moment against the doorway

11

which now shone bright yellow, as the fire gained momentum. They didn't stop but ran down the street behind Eddie, who, as soon as they rounded the corner, forced them to slow to a casual walk. "Good, Lightnin'!" Eddie said, as soon as he could catch his own breath. "That's the fastest I've ever seen you move! Guess we'll just have to build a fire under you to get you in motion from now on!" And Chico laughed and clapped him on the back.

When they reached the building Eddie's family lived in, he said, "Come on up. My old man and lady will still be working, and my brother's over at his club, working on that dumb car. We'll have the place to ourselves." The entry door was just closing behind them, when the first fire sirens could be heard in the distance.

The stairwell stank of stale urine and vomit, but the boys were used to it and didn't notice. Eddie's family's apartment was clean on the inside — his mother obviously made an effort — but the furnishings were old and threadbare. In fact, the only new thing in sight was the television set, and that Eddie flicked on as he passed it on the way to the kitchen. Making straight for the refrigerator, he called out, "Hey, we're in luck! My old man left some beer! He'll be mad as hell when he gets back, but let him do something about it. I'm too big for him to mess around with anymore." He brought back three cans and settled down in front of the tube, passing a can to each of the others. They watched the last half-hour of a Mod Squad re-run, and then the six o'clock news was on.

"The top news story this evening is a four-alarm fire now in progress in the south Bronx. Channel 7's mobile unit is there, and fire trucks are still arriving. . ." On the screen, an entire city block was on fire, with trucks and hoses everywhere, and police setting up a barrier to hold back the crowds of onlookers and make an avenue for the firefighting equipment. Channel 7's on-the-scene reporter was interviewing the fire chief, who was obviously resentful of the interruption and anxious to get back to fighting the fire.

"Chief, they tell me this blaze is less than an hour old; how did it get started?"

"God only knows! With these old buildings, anything could touch them off. City ought to tear them down!" He turned his back on the camera. "Harry, get number four up here, on the double!"

"Uh, chief?" And the fire chief turned around, scowling. "Do you suspect arson?" the reporter asked.

"How the hell do I know?" And he turned away again. "No, no, no! Move the ladder team down to the end. Get some water on that roof!"

And with the promise of fuller coverage on the eleven o'clock news, the newsroom went on to its next story. Eddie was stunned, the beer in his hand forgotten. "Did you see that? That was our fire!"

"Yeah!" said Chico, watching Eddie, to see how he should react. The younger boy, whose name was Raul, said nothing; but he did not seem very happy.

13

"You know," Eddie was saying, "if those TV guys are going to stay there and cover that fire, they're going to be interviewing bystanders, especially anyone who saw it in the beginning ..." Suddenly, he jumped up. "Come on, you guys, we're gonna be on TV!"

"Are you crazy?" protested Raul. "That's the *last* place you want to be!"

"No, man," said Eddie, pulling on his old parka, "it's the *first*! You heard the man say they don't have any idea how it got started. Well, maybe we'll give them a phony clue." He pulled on his gloves and nodded at Chico to do the same. "'Sides, how often you ever gonna get a chance to be a star?"

"Count me out," said Raul with unaccustomed firmness.

Eddie looked at him closely and saw that he was serious. "Aw, go home to your mama, glue-sniffer!" he said disgustedly. "When you grow up enough to be a man, you're welcome to travel with us. Let's go, Chico, we got a TV appointment." And the three of them parted company.

When he got home, his mother was in the living room of their apartment, in her easy chair, watching television. Raul took off his jacket and hung it on the peg next to the door, then wandered around the perimeter of the room, looking at the banner from Niagara Falls, the rose crystal candy dish his father had given his mother on their tenth anniversary, the last year he was home. He drifted over to the shelves with the

14

china dog and the tea cup and saucer and the polished wooden box with pins in it, and on to the photograph of his brother when he was little, taken at Coney Island. "Where's Felipe?" he asked idly coming over and sitting down on his end of the sofa.

"Over at Fox Street, watching the fire, like everyone else." She looked at him. "Didn't you hear about the fire?"

"Yeah, I heard," he said, off-handedly. He became conscious of her scrutiny. "Mama, why are you looking at me that way for?"

"Raul, is something wrong?"

"Why? What could be wrong?" and he turned back to the television.

"With you, I always know when something's wrong. Not with your brother, but with you, I can tell. And I can tell it now."

"Look, Mama," he said, exasperation creeping into his voice, "nothing's wrong! Now watch the show." And he turned resolutely toward the tube.

She let it alone for awhile, but she was worried, and she couldn't keep it inside indefinitely. At the next commercial, she started again. "Raul, are you on something? You know, taking something?"

"Mama, I'm not taking anything! Now will you let me watch this?" And he again turned back to the television set, which at that moment was showing another commercial.

"You remember what Felipe told you," she persisted, a tremor in her voice. "If he ever caught you using marijuana or heroin, he'd beat you up so bad, you couldn't even hold the stuff in your hand!"

15

"That Methadone junkie!" Raul exploded, "who's he to talk? So now he gets his fix courtesy of the government, what —"

"Don't you talk that way about your brother!" his mother shouted back at him. "You wait until Friday night, when George gets here. He'll take the strap to you!"

"My weekend father," said Raul bitterly. "Your man doesn't dare show his face around here during the week, for fear the welfare worker will catch him, and it'll cost you your benefits. Christ, what a way to live!"

"Why you ungrateful little —"

Suddenly Raul waved her to silence; the eleven o'clock news had just come on, and the lead story was again the fire. "Jack," the field reporter was saying to the newscaster back in the studio, "I've got a young man here who claims to have an idea of how the fire might have gotten started." The camera shifted to the figure standing next to the reporter; it was Eddie.

"Well, like I was saying," Eddie grinned into the camera, "there's a lot of rubbish in those old buildings. Maybe some glue-sniffers were in there, havin' a party, and one of them dropped a match, or something? You know, it could happen so easy —" The reporter abruptly thanked him, but before the camera moved away to follow a ladder crew manning a hose, it caught a glimpse of a hard-eyed patrolman in the background, listening.

Later that night, there was a knocking at the apartment door. Raul, who had not been able to sleep, looked at his watch: it was three in the morning.

16

2

The Black Hat Bandit

"Honey, how come you never told me how you got this?" purred the long, lithe black girl, as she stretched in bed and traced the scar on the face of the man next to her, with a ruby fingernail.

"You never asked me, baby," said the well-muscled young man, taking her hand away and turning his head away on the pillow, to indicate that the conversation was terminated.

"Well, I'm asking now," she said playfully. "I want to hear the whole story," and she walked two fingers up the rise of his massive shoulder and over towards his face.

"There's nothin' to hear. I was in a gang when I was younger, before I got sent to the joint. The gang got in a rumble. Some punk cut me with a razor. No big deal."

"Is that how come they call you Razor?"

"No. They call me that, because now I carry one, too. And they know I've used it a time or two." He got up. "Now I got to get goin' — got work to do."

She stretched again and pulled the sheet tight around her, so that it outlined her figure. "You sure you want to leave old Sal just now, Mr. Razor Daniels?"

He looked at her, his eyes cold. "It's two o'clock, and that bank closes at three, baby." He pulled on jeans, a black turtleneck, a denim jacket, socks and boots. Then, from under the bed he pulled a black leather suitcase. Some dust came along with it, and he brushed it away in disgust. "Don't you ever clean this place?" And he looked around at the dirty clothes, the overflowing trash baskets, the windows so sooty that it seemed gray out, even when it wasn't. Not that there was anything to see, other than the air shaft in the back, and the fire escape of the building next door.

"Listen!" Sal hissed. "You want to make an honest woman out of me? Get us a place for me to set up house in, and I'll keep it slick as a whistle. Meantime, keep your observations to yourself!"

He looked at her, took a step towards her, then changed his mind and opened the suitcase, taking out a wide-brimmed black hat, a brightly-colored Mexican serape, and a long-barreled Colt .44, that must have been at least a century old. Standing in front of Sal's full-length mirror, he carefully folded the serape long and narrow and put it over his left shoulder, like a matador dressing before a bullfight. Next, he donned the black hat, pulling it down low over his eyes. He turned to the left and the right, checking his profile.

18

Kneeling on the bed behind him, Sal giggled. "All you need now is one of those long, thin cigars," she said, her voice playful again. He picked up the heavy revolver, pulled back the hammer, and spun the cylinder. "Where on earth did you get that thing, Sugar?" she asked.

He smiled. "Won it from an actor in a poker game. He stole it from a movie studio." He let the hammer fall with a loud *click*. "Couldn't find any bullets that would fit it. Just as well; I'd probably blow somebody away if it were loaded, get me thirty-five, fifty, a hundred years for stick-up murder."

"You gonna take on a whole bank by yourself with an unloaded gun?" Sal said, amazed. "You gotta be plumb outa your head!"

"No, baby. Whitey's gonna be so scared, he's gonna do exactly as I ask." Sal stopped smiling when she heard the menace in his tone.

"But why the crazy get-up?" she asked, suddenly serious. "You couldn't be more conspicuous if you tried."

"That's the whole point," he said quietly, sticking the long-barreled .44 in his belt, out of sight under his denim jacket. "All they're gonna see is this here serape and hat and cannon. They'll probably call me the Black Hat Bandit. But as for a physical description, wouldn't surprise me if they didn't even notice I was black." He glanced at his watch; it was 2:20. "I better split."

"Tell me one other thing," Sal said, getting off the bed and draping a sheet around her, as she crossed the room to him. "Why do you have to go all the way uptown to Madison and 65th to rob

19

a bank? Why can't you just rob one around here?"

" 'Cause down here I'm known; I wouldn't get two blocks before some stoolie would drop a dime on me. 'Sides, I do a job down here, whitey's not gonna think nothin' of it. I do a job up there, where the richest whiteys do their banking, and they're gonna be scared — plenty scared!" And he took off the serape and hat and put them and the gun back in the suitcase.

"Well, hurry back, or I just might not be here."

"You'll be here, Sal," he said quietly. "You don't start until six. But you'd be here anyway, if I told you."

"Don't be too sure —"

With his left hand he grabbed her wrist and twisted it behind her back, while his right whipped a straight razor out of his hip pocket, flipped it open, and pressed the cutting edge against her forehead. It took less than a second. Sal's eyes widened with terror, her neck cords standing out with the effort not to move. For the tiniest movement would mean a permanent gash. "I'm sure, baby," he whispered, and just as quickly released her, and went out the door.

Walking to the nearest subway, he caught the local IRT, and rode to 68th Street. Waiting for the rest of the pedestrians to leave the platform, he opened the suitcase and put on the hat and serape, tucking the .44 in his belt, out of sight under his jacket. With that, he strolled up the platform, up the subway stairs, and out into the sidewalk traffic. It was a sunny afternoon in early June, and the warmth of that first truly summery day had brought many shoppers out. For all his outlandish garb, he attracted few backwards looks; after all, this was New York, where the unusual was hardly unusual at all. He was just another flakey dude, living out some harmless fantasy.

He arrived at the bank at two minutes to three. The guard was already standing by the door with the key in his hand. Daniels pulled the brim of his hat so low that his eyes were barely visible beneath it, and slipped inside. The bank was empty of customers, and the guard looked impatiently at him, as he locked the door behind him. Daniels walked purposefully over to the receptionist's desk, behind which sat an attractive blonde girl of about nineteen in a beige cashmere sweater. "Yes, sir, may I help you?"

Daniels leaned over her desk and looked her directly in the eyes. "*I'm gonna kill you!*" he whispered slowly, relishing each word and never taking his eyes from hers. He watched her eyes widen and her mouth start to open, and his gaze sharpened. He eased the denim jacket back, enought to reveal the butt of the revolver at his waist. Any thought of screaming left her; she stared at him, transfixed in terror. "Call the manager to come over here," he whispered. "Tell him there's a gentleman here to see him. And if you let anything come into your voice that tips him off, it'll be the last thing you ever say."

Unable to look away, she reached forward for the intercom, pushing the top button. "Mr. Haskel, could you come to the reception desk?

There's a gentleman here to see you."

"What is it, Connie? It's after closing."
Daniels let her know through his eyes that her life
depended on the next words out of her mouth.

"He won't tell me, except that it's important."

"Very well, I'll be there in a moment."

The door to an office in the back of the bank
opened, and a chubby younger man in a brown
three-piece suit emerged. He came up to the desk
briskly, intending to take care of whatever it was
and get the oddly dressed character on his way.
"Yes, what can I do for you?"

Daniels waited until he was close enough so
that no one else in the bank could see what was
happening, then he drew the .44 and stuck the tip
of its barrel under Mr. Haskel's double chin,
pressing it into the flesh. Taking his gaze from the
girl, who didn't move, he turned it to Mr. Haskel
and looked deep into his eyes, his face less than a
foot away. "If one person touches one button,"
he said quietly, "they're gonna have to repaint
the ceiling. 'Cause your brains are gonna be all
over it. Do you understand?" And he elevated his
chin slightly with the barrel and drew back the
hammer, letting him hear the sound of it. That
click, coupled with the smouldering hatred he saw
in Daniels' eyes, undid Mr. Haskel. In the
beginning, he had been scared but still in control
of himself. Now he believed.

"I want you to take a money bag and fill it with
all the bills behind the windows and the reserves
in the vault. No check, no change, and no trick or
marked money," he said, emphasizing the last.

"You have five minutes. But don't hurry. Because if anyone even suspects that anything's wrong, and the police come, we aren't gonna play no hostage games. We're gonna hold court right here. And the sentence will be carried out on the premises. Now get movin', I'll keep the young lady company."

Mr. Haskel went to the vault, returned with a money bag, and stopped behind each of the windows. At the last window, a young teller, eager to make points, said, "Can I help you, Mr. Haskel?"

For a fraction of a second he hesitated, but a glance over at the reception desk, where Daniels was watching his every move, convinced him. "No, Miss Perkins, that won't be necessary. But thank you," he added, giving her a smile.

When he returned to the reception desk, Daniels, the gun back in his belt, out of sight, put the suitcase on the desk and opened it, and Mr. Haskel put the money bag inside. "Now," said Daniels, "I want you to escort me to the door. And I want you to say, loud enough for the guard to hear it, 'Good afternoon, Mr. Johnson, come and see us again.' " Daniels paused and went on slowly. "And if you don't say it just right, I'll kill you. *And* the guard." He nodded, and the two of them walked to the front door.

Seeing them approach, the guard unlocked the door and held it open for Daniels. "Good afternoon, Mr. Johnson," Mr. Haskel said, in a clear voice, "come and see us again." Daniels nodded and went out the door. A few doors down Madison, he ducked into an office building, took

23

the first elevator up, and got off at the first stop.
Going around the corner to his left, where he
knew the stairs would be, he opened the fire door,
and went into the deserted stairwell. He glanced
at his watch: it was a quarter past three. Taking
off the hat and the serape, he put them into the
suitcase with the .44, alongside the money bag,
and took out a purple beret and lavender scarf.
Putting on the beret at a rakish angle, he tied the
scarf around his neck, cowboy style. Going back
out in the corridor, he rang for a down elevator
and soon emerged on the street, putting just a
hint of swish into his walk. He attracted hardly a
backward glance — just another flakey faggot,
living out some harmless fantasy ....

He crossed at the light, just as three patrol cars
came screaming up Madison.

But when he reached Sal's apartment, his cool
vanished. She was shaking with fear. "What is
it?" he said to her.

"Your parole officer was just here. Someone
had tipped him you were stayin' here, and he said
he was gonna put you in violation of parole for
not checkin' in with him. And that he'd be back
with a warrant." She gave in to the fear that was
rising up in her. "You're hot, honey! And they
don't even know about the bank yet!"

Before Daniels could reply, there was a knock
at the door. "You haven't seen me," Daniels
whispered, throwing the bag under the bed.
"Keep that for me, and shut the window behind
me, before you open the door." There was

24

another knock, louder, as Daniels raised the window and ducked out onto the fire escape.

Climbing to the roof, he went to the front of the building and looked cautiously over the side. Down below, a squad car was parked in front of the building, with a policeman waiting, and another entering the alley. He gauged the distance to the next building — about nine feet. Backing up, he took a run and leapt across the alley, making the other roof with inches to spare. The door to the roof was locked, but the next building was closer, and he made it with no difficulty. That roof door was open, and soon he was out on the street, strolling along with his hands in his pockets — and no place to go.

3

The Drifter

Keith yawned and gazed out the window of his bedroom at the beautifully manicured, deep green lawn that stretched away for three acres before it reached the little brook that bordered their property on the south side. Through the open window, he could hear the droning, humming sounds of summer. A sparrow darted by, and he idly watched its flight, as it dropped down next to the pool, walked over to the footbath, and plopped in to douse its feathers. The reflection of the sun on the surface of the pool was dazzling, and as he watched, a hint of a breeze rippled the surface, creating a million tiny suns. Keith gazed at it absently for several minutes, then looked at the brass ship's clock on his desk. It was three o'clock.

He turned his attention to the paper in front of him. It was a job application, the third he had filled out that week. Name: Keith R. Lawson, Jr. Address: 10 Basking Ridge Road, Far Hills, New Jersey. Age: 17. Education: Far Hills Country

Day School, 1966-74; Lawrenceville Academy, 1974-78 . . . He put the ball-point pen down, and gazed back out the window. Then he got up and began to wander through the empty house. He smiled as he entered Kathy's room; there were horses everywhere — little porcelain and crystal horses on her bureau and desk, on her night table a larger plastic horse that she had made herself from a kit, on the wall there were framed prints of horses, and taped to the closet and bathroom doors were posters of horses jumping. "You're right, Sis," he murmured, "they *are* nicer than people." On his way out, he admired the show ribbons adorning a lampshade; most of them were blue. "Not bad for only thirteen," he said.

At the end of the upstairs hall was the master bedroom. He hesitated for a moment, then went in. On the wall, next to his father's closet, hung several documents and photos. Keith knew them by heart, but he studied them as if for the first time. There was the diploma from Lawrenceville, just like the one in the bottom drawer of his desk, only his father's was dated 1951. And the one from Princeton, 1955. There was a commission in the Navy, also 1955, and the Harvard Business School diploma, class of '60. There were citations from the various companies he had worked for, most recently the Rahway Belt Company, of which he had been president for the past five years.

And then there were the photographs: his father in a Lawrenceville football uniform with a big smile, holding a game ball. His father in a crew shirt with a wide diagonal stripe, standing in a row with seven other tall men, each holding up a long oar by his side. His father's long, lean face beneath a white officer's hat, very serious, and another, in flying gear, on the wing of a Navy carrier jet, grinning. His father at his skeet club, holding his English shotgun at the ready, his eyes, hidden behind aviator's sunglasses, on the high house. His father, shaking hands with President Ford.

Keith's face registered nothing. He opened the door to his father's closet, glanced at the soft cashmere sportcoats, and ran a finger over the familiar ties with the little gamebirds and racquets on them. His finger stopped at a newer, brighter striped tie. Raising his eyebrows, he lifted the tie off the rack, folded it neatly, and stuck it in his hip pocket.

He closed the closet door and went downstairs, drifting into the library. The room was small enough to be cozy and was paneled in cherrywood and lined with bookshelves that mostly contained the bestsellers his parents had read over the years. Above the mantel was an oil painting of a hunting dog, and a gallery of family photos adorned his mother's antique desk. There was a big bay window, overlooking the same vista that Keith's room did, and it was flanked on the left by his father's gun cabinet, and on the right by his father's deep, overstuffed easy chairs. On the sofa opposite were scatter pillows, needlepointed by his mother, and next to the sofa, set in the wall behind two folding paneled doors, was the bar.

Cocking his head and listening to the stillness for a moment, Keith went to the doors and opened them. Row upon row of different-sized glasses met his eyes, some with hunting dogs on them, some with gamebirds, some with monogrammed initials. Because there was a mirror behind them, it seemed like there were twice as many as were actually there, and Keith selected a short, fat, round one. Reaching for the vodka among the cluster of bottles on the bar's counter, he held it up to the light, as if he were a connoisseur of fine wine, examining the label of a vintage Bordeaux. As it turned out, he was examining the label and located a tiny pencil mark at its edge, which matched the level of the vodka inside. Smiling, he set the bottle down and opened a door under the counter, taking some ice from the machine concealed there.

His action disturbed the ice machine, which now noisily activated itself — and covered the sound of the garage door opening. Putting the ice in the glass, he filled it nearly to the brim with vodka, then turned on the bar sink's tap to the thinnest of trickles and carefully refilled the bottle back up to the mark at the edge of the label. So intent was his concentration that he did not notice, in the mirror behind the glasses, the face of his mother watching him. He screwed the top back on the vodka bottle and carefully replaced it so that it was facing in the same direction in which it had been. That done, he sighed and gratefully raised the glass to his lips — and over its rim met his mother's gaze in the mirror.

If he was surprised, he didn't show it. He took a swallow, then turned around. "Congratulations, Mother," he said, smiling, "you've caught me."

Shock, grief, and despair flashed across his mother's face. "I thought it was Alice," she said, for want of anything else to say. Alice was their live-in cook. "How — how long has this been going on?" she managed.

"For about a year. I'm surprised you didn't notice sooner." He waited for her to say something, but she was speechless. "Now that you know," he said, "I suppose you're going to tell Dad?"

"Of course. He's going to be very upset to learn that his son is on his way to becoming an alcoholic. That is, if you're not already one." Keith winced. He noted that her eyes were brimming with tears and that she was fighting to control her emotions. He was sorry he had hurt her, but she had hurt him, too. And so he hurt her back. "Are you going to also tell him about the little drink you sometimes have yourself, to get ready for his coming home?"

"I won't stand for you talking to me that way!" she said, her eyes blazing.

"Oh, come off it, Mother; don't pull that holier-than-thou crap with me!"

Keith's mother walked up to him and slapped him across the face. The fingers of his left hand closed into a fist, then unclenched. Raising the glass in a silent toast to her, he downed its contents in one gulp, set it on the bar, and walked out of the room.

"Where are you going?"

"Out," he murmured, not caring whether she heard it or not.

31

Keith wandered down the rolling green lawn to the brook, where he sat down on a large, smooth rock and stared at the running water. He listened to the burbling of the brook, as it found its way over a rocky stretch like the rapids of a miniature river. After a while, he picked up a pebble and plunked it into the middle of a smooth place in the brook. Then, when the ripples had died away, he picked up another.

Two hours later, he heard his father in the distance, down-shifting as he approached their driveway. It was time to go in for dinner. With a sigh, he got up and went into the house. Everyone was already in the library when he got there. Keith glanced at his mother curled up on the end of the sofa, needlepointing under the light of a brass standing lamp. Her face was impassive, but she didn't look up at him. He couldn't tell whether she had told him yet or not. Kathy was lying on her stomach on the window-seat, doing her homework, her big, mod horned-rims perched on the end of her nose. His father was at the bar, making himself and his mother a drink. He had just finished as Keith came in the room, and greeted Keith with a cheery "Hello!"

So she hadn't told him. "Hi, Dad," Keith smiled back.

"Did you get that job application finished?" his father asked, as he handed his mother a gin-and-tonic.

"Yup," Keith lied, "I'll take it over there first

thing in the morning," he added, buying himself enough time to get it done.

"You'd better get a haircut first," his father said, smiling, but meaning it. Keith ran his hand through his long blond hair and said nothing, but the mood in the room was no longer as cheerful as it had been.

"How did it go at work today?" his mother asked brightly.

"Oh, the usual," his father replied. "Bart thinks the union will settle without a walkout, if we meet their pension demand."

"Are you going to?" said his mother, sincerely interested.

"I think so. We can't afford to shut down just when we need to build up our inventory, and they know it. We'll just —"

"Can I have a drink?" Keith asked, interrupting.

"You can have a beer," his father said, looking at him.

"I'd like a real drink, Dad, like you and Mother." He avoided looking at his mother.

"We've been all through that. The only reason we let you have a beer with us, is so that you'll do your drinking at home. You're not old enough to know how to handle hard liquor. In fact, after what happened last spring, I'm surprised you have the temerity to ask for a drink at all."

"Dad, all I had was a few beers at a party!"

"And got picked up for driving while intoxicated on that motorcycle of yours, and drinking under age, and with a marijuana reefer in your pocket!"

33

"You've got that charge sheet memorized, haven't you?" Keith shot back.

"Maybe *you* ought to memorize it!" his father said. "It's your single outstanding achievement to date. It's too bad you're not as interested in getting a job, as you seem to be in getting a drink. It doesn't have to be at Rahway Belt. Any job! But since you refuse to go to college —"

"Here it comes," Keith murmured, "the old okey-doke."

"I'm willing to pay your way anywhere; it doesn't have to be Princeton. There are a lot of kids in this country who would give their eye teeth to have their way paid through college, but —"

"— you haven't got a grateful bone in your body," Keith finished the sentence for him. "I know, you've tallied my ungrateful bones a million times," he said, getting to his feet, aware that he had finally overstepped that invisible line. His father stood up, too. In all their "discussions", Keith's mother had never allowed it to go this far, and both of them were almost regretful that it had happened. But it was too late now.

"It's about time you learned that the world doesn't owe you a living, young man!" And there was a set to his jaw that indicated imminent action.

"Yes, maybe it is about time," said Keith evenly, his face two feet from his father's. "And incidentally, I *can* handle hard liquor. I've been handling yours for over a year now. Ask Mother, if you don't believe me." Surprised at this development, his father turned to his mother.

"I caught him at it this afternoon," she said.

34

"I was going to tell you about it after Kathy had gone to bed."

"That's right. I could get a very nice high on in the afternoons, while Mother was at the club or having one with her bridge friends. I wondered when you were going to notice that your booze was getting a little weak. But with your two drinks before dinner and all the entertaining you do, none of the open bottles were around here long enough for you to notice."

"Why you—"

But before he could say or do anything, Keith spun on his heel and walked out of the room.

"*Come back here!*" his father commanded.

"Go to hell!" Keith yelled, as he slammed out the garage door. The far door to the spacious three-car garage was open, and in the twilight, he could just make out his mother's Continental and his father's Porsche 911, neither of which he was allowed to drive. Farthest over was the family's compact station wagon, which his mother used for errands, and which he was allowed to use for dates. He walked quickly by it, to where his big, jet-black Kawasaki 900 waited. He jumped on the kick-starter, and it rumbled to life, just as the door to the house opened, and a shaft of yellow light pierced the garage.

"Keith!" his father shouted. "You get your — " But the rest of his words were lost in a deafening roar, as Keith revved up his bike and blasted out of the garage.

Ten minutes later, he turned in the driveway of a home in Bernardsville. The garage door was open, and there was a light on inside. Under the light, a boy approximately his own age was working on a motorcycle. "Andy!" called Keith, dismounting. "Man, am I glad you're home! Are you going to have that thing together soon enough for us to do some riding?"

Andy straightened, wiped his hands on a rag, and scratched his head. "I don't think so, man. It's gonna be another couple of hours, at least."

"Oh. Thought we'd run over to Morristown, see what's going on. Maybe hoist a few. I need to get some miles under me."

"Well, my dad's got some beer in the fridge, help yourself," and he jerked his thumb in the direction of a refrigerator in the corner of the garage, and returned to his work.

Keith went to it and opened the door. "You want one?" he called.

"No, thanks," Andy said, reaching for a socket wrench, "just had dinner. Say," he said, "don't your folks eat about this time? What, did you have a run-in with them?"

"Yeah, that's why I wanted to do some riding." He took a long pull on the can.

"You hungry?" Andy asked.

"Nope. Thirsty, though. You mind if I have another?"

"Help yourself," shrugged Andy, turning back to his machine. "You know where it is."

Three hours later, Andy stood up stiffly. "Finished," he said, satisfied. Then he looked at Keith. "You look pretty well finished, too. Want me to drive you home?"

"Not going home," Keith said, slurring his words.

"Well, what are you planning on doing?"

"Stay here with you."

"No way, man," Andy said, shaking his head. "My parents are friends with your parents; all hell will break loose."

"Then I think I'll just hit the road," Keith said, getting a little shakily to his feet.

"Can't let you do it, man," Andy said, taking his arm. "Look, you can stay here, but you're not going riding. You've killed a couple of six-packs, and you're likely to kill yourself, too."

"Didn't know you were counting!" Keith said, jerking his arm free.

"Man, you gotta stay off that bike!" Andy said, grabbing his arm again.

"Leggo me! Nobody's gonna tell me what to do, not you, not nobody!" And Keith, who was a good deal bigger and stronger, pushed Andy away from him, sending him crashing back into his own bike, which collapsed under his weight.

Holding his beer can carefully, Keith swung into the saddle, kicked the starter, and thundered off into the night, without so much as a backward look. As he turned up the street, he remembered to turn on his headlight. "Fresh air will straighten me out," he said aloud, but all it did was make him a wide-awake drunk.

Fortunately, there was little traffic in the Jersey foothills at that hour of the night, and he found that by staying in the very middle of the road, he could manage to negotiate the winding curves. He laughed, as he finished the can of beer and flung it into the night sky. He was on Hardscrabble Road now, heading for Mendham. It was a narrow, twisting wooded road, with blind corners, and he noticed a glow ahead, signaling the approach of an oncoming car. Keith backed down on the gas and made an attempt at getting over to his side of the road, just as the car came around a corner. There was the sound of brakes squealing and then a loud horn, as the car swerved to get out of his way.

"Big car!" Keith said. "Thinks he needs the whole road." Then he laughed again. "Must have thought I was a puhdiddle," he said, using his father's expression for a car with only one headlight working.

Another car approached, this time on a straight-away. Even so, Keith's course was sufficiently erratic for the driver of the car to slow way down and then stand on his horn, the sound of it rising and then falling away, as they passed.

Now the lights of Mendham could be seen up ahead, and Keith slowed, but only to forty, so that he still had to lean way over to make the corner into the main street. He didn't notice the police car parked in the gas station with its lights out, nor that those lights flicked on just after he passed. He headed out of town to the north, turning up Cold Hill Road, which had its own share of treacherous places. Another car was coming, and once again Keith was in the middle of the road. But this time he made no attempt to pull over. "Let 'em get outa *my* way, for a change!" he said.

The car honked its horn a couple of times, then

at the last minute swung hard to the right, and plunged off the road into a drainage ditch, coming to a stop as it crashed into a pine tree. It all happened so quickly that Keith didn't register it, at first. Then he did and slowed and swung his machine around. The car's hood was steaming, completely stove in, in the center, and there was no movement from inside the car.

Keith got off his bike, and walked over to the car. Inside, an older man was slumped forward, restrained by his shoulder harness, his head lolling on his chest. "Mister?" Keith called and was about to open the door, when he heard another car approaching, a blue light circling on its roof.

Panicking, Keith ran back to his bike, jumped on it, and sped off. But when the police car started its siren, he backed off and pulled over.

The policeman approached him warily, his revolver drawn, a flashlight in his other hand. "I've been following you, since you came through town. Do you realize you may have killed a man back there?"

"Oh, God!" Keith said, and he started to cry.

4

Three in the Morning

I was sitting in my office at 444 Clinton Avenue, leaning back in my chair and enjoying a quiet cup of hot chocolate before Monday morning got into high gear. In a few minutes, the phone would start ringing, and a steady stream of people would be calling or coming in with questions. But for the moment, it was blessedly peaceful. The early morning sun had already warmed the Brooklyn streets to a pleasant 75 degrees, and now it was filtering through the window, and falling on some of the books on the shelf near my desk. One of them was *The Cross and the Switchblade*, and now I picked it up and idly thumbed through it, remembering how it had all begun, some twenty years before. Dear Lord, was it *that* long ago?

My brother David had been a young pastor in a small rural church in central Pennsylvania, when he got fed up with watching late-night television every night, after his wife and children had gone to sleep. David was never one for half-way measures: he sold the television set and

41

committed himself to spending those two hours late at night in prayer and waiting before the Lord — every night. It was a difficult discipline, and it revealed a number of things to him about himself and his relationship with God. Then one night, he happened to notice in a copy of *Life* magazine, a news story about a bunch of teenage gang members who had been arrested in Brooklyn and would soon be arraigned in district court. Incredibly, the Lord seemed to be saying to him that he was to go there and help them!

All his logic dictated that to do anything of the sort was nothing short of insanity. What on earth could he, an obscure country preacher, do for those boys? Nothing, his head told him, except make a fool of himself. But in his heart, he sensed that God was calling him to trust Him, no matter what it cost his pride, and in these past weeks of waiting and praying, he had determined to trust God implicitly. So in the end, he listened to his heart. Bible in hand, he went into New York City, into the courtroom where the boys were being arraigned — and into a front-page *Daily News* photo of the Judge expelling him from the courtroom. The obscure country preacher was obscure no longer.

That was a hard time for David. Our parents were mortified; his friends thought he had flipped. But he hung in there, and God began to honor his obedience: the gang members knew that he had tried to help them, and knew that it had cost him. So they listened to him, where they might not have listened to anyone else. And they heard that Jesus Christ gave His life for them; He loved them that much. And it began to get to some of them.

Israel, one of the gang leaders, was one of the first to come under the conviction of the Holy Spirit, as David began to preach in the streets of Brooklyn. He knelt down there on the sidewalk, and let David pray for him, accepting Jesus into his heart, as his Lord and Savior. But not Nicky. Short, quick and wiry, Nicky Cruz was not buying any of that God stuff that day! The switchblade was far mightier than the cross back then.

But, as David would later often say, God had everything under control. I had joined him by then. The call that God had put on his life, He now put on mine also, to support the work that David was doing, in every way that I could. I took a sip of hot chocolate and smiled at the recollection of those early street services, with the American flag and the trumpet — brother, were we green! But God blessed our feeblest endeavors mightily.

And then came the night at St. Nick's boxing arena which changed everything. David had rented that barn of a place for a youth rally, and talk about green — if I had known what I do today, I would have gone in there with fear and trembling. As it was, I went blithely in, confident that the Lord's work was being done. The place was largely empty, and there were street gangs scattered all over, bantering and milling around and carrying on, while some church's youth choir tried valiantly to establish something approaching a reverent atmosphere. It was a tough assignment; the gangs were making fun of the choir and throwing taunts at one another, and the general effect was sheer chaos.

The program began with a couple of preliminary testimonies, which nobody seemed to be listening to, and by that time my own spirit was so down that I didn't realize I was already witnessing a miracle: *not one of those kids had left*. And when David got up to speak, there was such an anointing, that everyone in the place quieted down and listened. He didn't speak more than fifteen minutes, a very simple message on the love of God, from John 3:16. God so loved the world that He gave His only Son . . . That's how much He loves you. He wants to put His love in you, so that Italians can love Puerto Ricans, and Puerto Ricans can love Italians ... At that point, one Puerto Rican youth jumped up and started shouting in Spanish, pointing at a scar on his throat and then gesticulating over at a gang of Italians. But incredibly, his buddies pulled him back down into his seat, and he was still. David concluded, and his message got through.

When he finished and asked if anyone wanted to come forward and commit his life to Christ, I just about fell out of my chair when Nicky and Israel led their entire gang forward. And that conversion took; Nicky, who had been one of the most ruthless street leaders I had ever met, went on to become a dedicated street soldier for the Lord, as he describes so well in his book, *Run Baby Run*. Others followed his lead, and that night at St. Nick's marked the beginning of Teen Challenge.

I chuckled as I finished the hot chocolate; we didn't even know what a drug addict was in those days. We thought we had been called into the Bedford Stuyvesant area of Brooklyn where the gang wars were the worst, in order to show them that Christ's love, not war, was the answer. But scarcely had we gotten started, than heroin became the thing on the streets, and gangs started breaking up, as more and more members started turning their violence inward, on themselves, and began spacing out on dope. In heroin, we found that we were up against a much more powerful weapon of hell than we had ever faced before, and that young people whom we were leading to the Lord were falling back the very next day. What we needed, we came to realize, was a place where we could provide twenty-four-hour residential care for a sustained period — something that the sociological cure centers had known for some time. Thus the house at 416 Clinton became the first Teen Challenge center, and it and our relatively new, two-story building next door at 444 continued to function as the pilot model for the more than fifty such centers in cities all over the world.

It was ironic that now, twenty years later, we were going through a new transition phase: though heroin was still a grave problem, it no longer rated as the number one addiction problem in America today. Teenage alcoholism had surpassed it. And those kids who were doing dope were now much more difficult to help, because they had become poly-drug users, taking heroin *and* cocaine together, qualudes and barbituates, pyrobenzamine and talwins, red devils and angel dust. They would come into our crisis center so strung out that they couldn't remember what they took, and it was almost impossible to diagnose it.

We were once again in a whole new ballgame, having to learn a new set of rules, for we were now taking in as many alcoholics as addicts. But we had the same Holy Spirit showing us the way, and this time we had twenty years of experience working with addictive personalities under our belts. We had quickly learned, for instance, that the young alcoholic was a different breed of cat from the young addict, he came more often from middle class homes than welfare ghettos, and he turned to his thing more out of boredom than despair. In some ways he was easier to reach — unlike the addict, who constructed a cocoon of untouchable interior space around himself — but harder to cure: the young alcoholic often had difficulty accepting that his condition was that serious. He was a master at conning the people who were attempting to help him, and the person he was most successful at conning was himself. Either he had to have done something so horrendous that there was no avoiding the consequences of his addiction, or the hassles of parents, family and others outweighed the pleasure of drinking — or both.

And of course, getting him to a point where he actually *wanted* to be cured was only the beginning. Because in the final analysis, alcoholism was only a symptom, albeit an extremely destructive one, of a much deeper spiritual malaise. We had to find out what had

46

caused the alcoholic to start drinking in the first place, and deal with that, as led by the Spirit. And then finally, we had to make sure that the cured alcoholic did not develop a psychological dependency on the Teen Challenge program per se, but built up his dependency on the Lord Himself. I glanced over at the growing pile of manuscript pages on my desk; I would soon be publishing a book on teenage drinking which would document all of our findings ....

In the meantime, I had an idea for the next step that our crisis center might take, in its ongoing evolution, and I was anxious to try it out on Joe Revish, our intake supervisor. Joe was responsible for interviewing every inductee who wanted to enter the program, and he reported to Randy Larson, our program director, who in turn reported to me. Joe was permanently based at the Brooklyn center, while Randy and I divided our time between the Brooklyn office and its northern adjunct, Camp Champion, and I particularly valued Joe's input. I buzzed him on the intercom: "I've got a couple of ideas I'd like to get your reactions to sometime today, Joe; what does your interview schedule look like?"

"I've got three in the morning, but my afternoon is clear."

"Good. Suppose we get together after lunch then."

The contrast between the two could not have been more pronounced. Behind his desk sat Joe Revish, a husky, easy-going black man, with a relaxed way of asking questions and a note pad in front of him that was gradually filling with notes. On the other side of the desk sat a young, withdrawn Puerto Rican boy with a scraggly attempt at a moustache on his upper lip. The name at the top of Joe's note pad was Raul Castenada, and his age: 15.

"Before you went to jail, you lived with your mother, is that right?" Raul nodded. "And your father left home when you were six?" He nodded again. Joe asked more questions, filling in the canvas of his life, his patterns of behavior, his relationships with others his own age. The portrait that emerged was a sad one, of a boy who had been hurt so many times that he had lost touch with all his feelings — his subconscious had set up an emotional buffer zone to protect itself from any more hurt. His passivity was now almost complete.

"You were in jail, awaiting trial, when John Pagon of Pre-trial Services recommended that you come here?" Raul nodded. "What are the charges against you?"

"Twenty-one counts of arson." Joe whistled in spite of himself. "They say I burned down a whole block of tenements," Raul muttered.

"Did you?"

"What difference does it make? They say I did."

"Do you do dope?" Raul shook his head. "I sniffed glue sometimes," he volunteered.

"What are your feelings about coming here?"

Raul looked at him blankly, then said, "Mr. Pagon said that I could get a new life here." He

48

paused. "I think I'd like that. I don't have much of a life right now," and he smiled, embarrassed at the inadequacy of his answer.

"Okay," said Joe, "to enter the Teen Challenge program, which is a year long — four months in the induction phase, here and at Camp Champion, and eight months at the Farm — you are going to have to sign an agreement. At Teen Challenge we put a good deal of importance on a man's work. You are going to have to agree that, for the duration of your time in the program, you will not lay a hand on anyone in anger, you will act in a responsible manner in matters of self-control and self-discipline, you will not smoke or take drugs or use profanity, and so on," and he handed him the agreement typed on yellow paper. "But the thing is that you agree to cooperate at all times with the staff who are trying to help you. Read it carefully, and don't sign it, unless you are sure you want to." Raul did read it carefully and signed it without hesitation.

The next person in Joe's office was a decidedly different case. Bigger than Joe, and black, he brought with him an aura of intimidation. *Mr. Cool*, Joe wrote on his note pad. "Name?"

"Razor Daniels."

Joe shook his head, and smiled. "No, I mean your real name. We don't use street names here."

"My mother named me Raymond, but I haven't been called that in years."

"Okay, we'll just make it Ray. Age?"
"Twenty-four."

49

Joe sketched in the details of his background — father unknown, mother lived in Harlem, no other relatives, no fixed address, was living with girlfriend, two years in Attica for armed robbery — "What did you rob?"

"I knocked over some liquor stores uptown. But after two years in the joint, I ain't never gonna pull nothin' like that again! You been in there?" Joe shook his head. "Man, that place is a jungle! I don't want to tell you what woulda happened to me if I was any smaller!" He saw from Joe's expression that he was unimpressed. "Anyway, I made up my mind that I was goin' straight when I got out, and I have. Only now I started takin' dope and gettin' pretty —"

"Let me see your tracks," Joe interrupted him. Ray rolled back his sleeve. "You haven't been taking very much or doing it for very long," Joe said impassively.

"No, and that's why I want to quit now, while I still can. I ran into a Mr. Milton Delgado on the street, and he said that this was the place, and that Jesus was the man, if I wanted a high that would last a lifetime. So here I am."

"You say you left your girlfriend's just before you met Milton? Why did you leave?"

"Man, it wasn't my choice. She threw me out. Got herself another dude."

"You sure you're not just looking for three hots and a cot?"

"No, man," Ray said, grieved that Joe could so misunderstand him, "I need help, and I know it. My life ain't nothin' but a bunch of you know what. There's just got to be more to life than the scratchin' around I'm doin'. Your friend Milton thought I could find the answer here."

"Maybe you will," Joe said, tapping his chin with the pen, "maybe you just will." He took out an agreement form and explained it to him in detail. When he'd finished reading it, Joe looked him in the eye and said, "I want you to know that I know you're gaming it, all the way. I don't know what your game is yet, but it doesn't matter. God uses all sorts of ways to get us where He wants us." He smiled. "You've read the agreement; are you prepared to sign it?"

"Nothing would give me greater pleasure," Ray said, and borrowing Joe's pen, he signed his name with a flourish.

"Welcome to Teen Challenge," Joe said wryly.

"Thank you, man," grinned Ray, shaking his hand, "I know I'm going to like it here."

Keith Lawson was not at all sure that he would like it at Teen Challenge and told Joe so. But he also told Joe that it was the last chance for him, and he knew it. Matt Rocco, who was with the Essex County Probation Department, had heard of Keith's case — as had all of New Jersey, for the papers had gotten hold of it and had a field day. Matt had gone to talk to Keith and his mother, as soon as Keith was out on bail. He had told them about the Teen Challenge program, and that many young men who had been utterly without direction in their lives were able to chart a new, positive course there, by the grace of God, and with His help.

Keith had listened. He listened because he was scared — more scared than he had ever been in his life. Not because of all the charges that faced him, but because Mr. Henderson, the man who had run off the road trying to avoid him, had had a heart attack and was still in intensive care at Muehlenburg Hospital. And he listened because he knew in his heart that he could not go on the way he had been going. That alcohol alone would not do the job, and that the only thing that would was suicide. And he told that to Joe, too.

"Did Matt tell you that we're Pentecostals here, and that we look to God to do the healing, by his Holy Spirit, through the staff and prayer and the other individuals in the program?" Keith nodded. "Well, how do you feel about that?"

"I don't know. I never thought about God being real before. Especially not about Him really caring. I don't really understand it, but I don't mind it."

"You know," said Joe, "You're a pretty honest kid, when you get right down to it. You're going to do all right here."

Keith read over the agreement form and signed it, and then said, "One more question: What about my trial?"

Joe went down his notes. "Let's see: reckless driving, driving while intoxicated, drinking under age, all second offenses, plus leaving the scene of an accident, resisting arrest, and if Mr. Henderson dies, possibly negligent homicide — " Joe looked up, to see Keith put his head in his hands, and his shoulders begin to quake. He sensed that Keith's tears were not for himself but for the old man. "Well," Joe said, "that's something we can deal with right away." He made a note on a separate piece of paper. "We'll get Mr. Henderson on the top of our prayer list, and see if God won't take him off the critical list. And as for your trial," he said, "you can let God worry about that, too." Joe stood up. "You know, son, you may find that God is a whole lot more real than you realize."

5

A Group Called Genesis

On the stairs, leading Raul, Ray and Keith up to their room, was Charles Pucillo. A lanky, affable graduate of the program himself, Charles was doing a year's internship at the Brooklyn center, prior to going to Bible school. Reaching the top of the stairs, he showed them into a sunlit room that had two double bunks in it, immaculately made, two bureaus, a desk and chair, and a closet. "Be it ever so humble," said Charles, "this will be your home for the next week or two, until they have room for you at Camp Champion. So keep it neat and keep it real." And he went on without bothering to explain what he meant. "Get your stuff put away as quickly as possible and get downstairs for lunch. It's hamburgers," he added, and turned and went downstairs himself.

The three young men each gravitated to a bunk that the other two didn't seem interested in and started putting their belongings away. The job done, they left 416 Clinton and went to the dining hall in 444 where about twenty-five staff and students were already eating. The dining hall was cheerful and bright, and the decibel level was high, but Ray, Raul and Keith preserved the silence that had grown up between them, breaking it only to ask for the salt and pepper.

About that time, I came into the dining hall myself, and asked Dominick, our cook, if it was too late to get a hamburger. He had saved one for me, and I took it and some french fries and peas and chocolate cake over to where Joe was sitting with Charles, Don Richmond, another intern, and Hector Ruiz, the three leaders of Genesis, which was the name of the group into which new inductees went before they were transferred. "Those three over there," I nodded in the direction of the only three silent characters in the room, "are those your new inductees?"

Joe nodded. "The Puerto Rican came via John Pagon. He's got twenty-one counts of arson against him, but I think it's a bum rap. Anyway, John told me on the phone that the kid has been so long without love, he's forgotten what it feels like — if he ever knew. And that was my impression, too. When he tries to smile, it's enough to make you want to cry."

"What about the other two?" Don asked, since he would have them in class that afternoon.

"The black fellow is one of Milton's candidates. When I talked to Milton, he said the guy was probably fronting it, and I told Daniels to his face that I knew he was, but I get a funny feeling he's supposed to be here. The other guy was referred by Matt Rocco. He's at the end of his rope and badly shaken, which is good, because he's open. He's a drinker and has some pretty heavy charges facing him, but I don't think booze is his problem. Neither does Matt, who went to his home — a big place in Far Hills. The mother is a nice lady with class, but awfully uptight. The father couldn't be there on account of some business dinner."

Later, as Joe and I left to go to my office, he stopped by their table and introduced me. Keith stood up, and the other two followed suit. "Well, are you getting settled in?" I asked, and they all nodded. "Good. We'll get you up to Camp Champion as soon as we can," I assured them, and they thanked me, without really knowing what for. A half-hour later, they began to find out.

Hector and Charles had an informal meeting then in one of the unused classrooms. Hector and Charles sat on the edge of the teacher's desk. The three newcomers had separated themselves from each other by a couple of desks each, and from the front as far as possible. "Come on up front," Hector said, and they did. "What this is, is a chance for you to ask questions, but mainly to get the lowdown on what you're in for." Keith and Raul laughed, and Hector continued.

"The Teen Challenge program lasts for a year, more or less — more, if you fight it; less, if there happens to be an opening at the Farm, and your group and the staff feel that you are ready to go."

"What's our group?" Keith asked.

"At Camp Champion, where you'll be for the better part of the next four months, you'll be in one of two groups — Alpha or Shekinah. You will eat together, work together, live in the same house together, worship together and work out your problems together. In short, you are going to learn how to live together as a family, something that a lot of people have never learned. Most of the guys who come here don't know the first thing about being sensitive to the needs of others, and I didn't either, when I first came to the program. But I'll tell you: you're going to learn. You are going to learn how to be open and honest with one another, and to get your real feelings out. You are going to learn what you do that hurts others, and how you can finally begin to have some peace in your heart, and — a lot of other things. But you'll be hearing more about that, when you get up there."

"In the meantime," said Charles, "you'll soon be joining a group called Genesis, which is composed mainly of guys like yourself, who are waiting to go to Camp Champion. Some of them have been waiting for more than a couple of weeks, because of an uncooperative or resistant attitude. We're giving them a chance to change. If they don't, they'll have to leave the program, because there's no way we can work with anyone who's going to be fighting us every step of the way."

"What if a person wants to leave the program?" Ray asked.

"They are free to, any time," Hector said. "This isn't jail; it's strictly a voluntary program. God wants to help you, and we want to help you. But God isn't in the business of twisting arms.

But if you split, and than change your mind," he said, looking at Ray, "you start all over again at the beginning, from day one. So remember that, when you're tempted to cut and run, as every one of you will be, at one time or another."

He looked at his watch. "The last eight months of the program will be spent at a Teen Challenge Training Center, and the one you'll be going to is located in Rehrersburg, Pennsylvania, the place we call the Farm, or 'God's Mountain'. There, you'll learn English composition or Spanish, as the case may be," he smiled at Raul, "how to express yourself logically and coherently on paper. And anyone who wants to study for high school equivalency exams will be helped to do so."

"What if someone has already been through high school?" asked Keith.

"You'll be surprised at how much you'll learn," Charles laughed. "You'll be taking courses like Money Management, Management of Time, the Gospels, How to Study, Foundations of Faith and so on. And the classroom is only half of your education curriculum. You'll get job experience, too, working in the print shop or the body shop, in the greenhouse or the waste water treatment plant. You'll — " but Hector cut him short, pointing to his watch. "And now," Hector said, "you'll meet the rest of Genesis group."

Don Richmond was just beginning his class, when Keith, Ray and Raul came in and took available desks. "Ah, here are the new men for Genesis," said Don, "making, let's see, eight in all. Why don't you new guys stand up and tell the rest of us who you are, and why you're here." There was a silence in the room, as each of the three was happy to let one of the others go first. "All right, we'll start with you," said Don, nodding towards Ray, who got to his feet.

"Razor — uh, *Ray* Daniels, and — what was the other part?"

"Why are you here?"

"Why am I here?" Ray repeated, stalling as long as possible. "I'm here, because I'm a user and an ex-con — I did two years for armed robbery — and I want to quit. And a fellow named Milton Delgado said that this was the place." He flashed a big grin, and Don turned to Raul, "Okay, now you."

"I don't know what to say, man. I'm Raul Castenada, and I was in jail awaiting trial for arson, and this amazing guy comes out of nowhere and says I should be here, and so here I am," and he sat down.

"Good," said Don, "and you?" He turned to Keith.

"Look, do I have to do this?"

"Yup. You're going to have to do a lot of things around here that you might not want to do, so you might as well make the best of it."

With a sigh, Keith got to his feet. "Keith Lawson. I was riding my bike, and I was drunk, and I caused an accident. A man talked to me about this place, and it sounded like where I ought to be."

"Okay, now the rest of you guys can introduce yourselves. You can skip the reasons why you're here." And they quickly went around the room. Among them were a cocky little Italian named Polo Ippolito, and a spacey, slow-talking boy named Larry Zonas, both of whom would be going to Camp Champion before the three new men.

Don now handed an eighteen-page booklet to each of the new men, entitled *A New Look at Life*. "This is the textbook that you'll need for this course. You'll go through it at your own pace, completing the assignments when you feel you're ready to. But you'll need to finish before you're due to transfer."

The booklet was simple in design, written in easy-to-understand language and amply illustrated, because many of the students who entered the program were barely literate. Don watched Keith as he thumbed through it with a condescending attitude at first, which soon changed as he saw that although the questions were easy to understand, they were very probing — in essence, calling the reader to weigh the meaning of his life and what he had done with it up to that point. And then it asked him to compare his life with a life that was Christ-centered.

Leaving Keith to ponder the booklet, Don went over to help one of the young men who had been in Genesis for more than a week. He was working on question #4: "How successful were you in doing what you had planned for your life?" And although he was talking to only one person, he knew that everyone else in the room was getting something out of it, too.

Afterwards, they went outside, where there was a basketball hoop and fooled around some, in a casual pick-up way. It turned out that Keith, who had played on his school team, had some pretty good moves; indeed, he was one of the most accomplished players in the group. But Ray was pretty good, too, and once when they went up together for a rebound, Ray gave him a shot with his elbow.

"Hey!" grunted Keith, "What are you doing? This isn't even a game!"

"Listen, whitey," Ray spat the words out. "I may have to live with you, but that sure don't mean I have to love you. You don't like the way I play, you just stay out of my way, you understand, honkey?"

It was the first time in his life that Keith had ever been on the giving or receiving end of such racial hatred, and he was completely nonplussed by it. He stood there, staring at Ray and not knowing what to do, until one of the other fellows said, "Hey, come on, you two, let's play ball." Play resumed, but without Keith, who sat down a little ways away and watched. And Ray, assuming that he had intimidated him, now played with a good deal of flamboyance, occasionally calling attention to himself when he sank a particularly stylish shot. A few of the guys seemed to appreciate him; most were turned off.

That evening, after supper, they had some free time, and they were encouraged to write home, if they had not been in touch in a while. Keith borrowed paper and pen and wrote:

Dear Mother and Dad,

It's going to be all right here. The staff are good men, they put it on the line, so you know where you're at. I met the director, Mr. Wilkerson, at lunch. He's kind of like a headmaster, mostly out of of sight. I'm in a room with a Puerto Rican named Raul who's younger than me, and a black guy named Ray who's older, and who has it in for me because I'm white. I think we're going to have to fight soon, because he's going to push me to it, and I'm not going to back down. We had a class in looking at your life, this afternoon. That may sound weird, but it made more sense than a lot of classes I've been in. My life didn't look so hot when I looked at it. I hope Mr. Henderson makes it.

> *Give my love to Kathy,*
> *Keith*

Raul's letter was even briefer, in Spanish, and Ray's began:

Baby —

Don't try to contact me here. I'll get in touch with you later. Just keep that bag under the bed nice and safe till I come for it, and keep yourself nice and safe for me, too . . . [the rest of the letter being too gamy to repeat here].

63

6

Walking in the Light

Tuesday morning dawned bright and early — a little too early for Keith, who had grown used to staying up late and sleeping late. But if one did not have a choice, then the trick was to stay as close to a state of somnambulance as possible. "While traveling in the Orient" (*i.e.* living in the dorm at boarding school), Keith had learned how to brush his teeth and get dressed while remaining almost totally asleep. In this fashion he could extend the night's merciful oblivion perhaps fifteen or twenty minutes into the morning, and once or twice he had made it all the way through breakfast. It wasn't much of an accomplishment, but in such trying circumstances as the present, the smallest victories mattered.

Raul, on the other hand, was one of those people who woke up like a light bulb turning on — *click*, and he was as wide awake as if he had been up for hours, and full of enthusiasm, too, before the demeaning realities of the day once again ground him into silence. This morning, he made more conversation in five minutes than he had in the previous twenty-four hours, and most of it in Keith's ear, since Ray seemed to regard him with bemused contempt. Unfortunately, the only thing Keith had not learned while traveling in the Orient, was how to answer questions while still, for all intents and purposes, asleep.

"Hey, man," said Raul, "what do you make of that tall dude, Charles Pucillo?"

"Two can ride a bicycle almost as cheaply as three," mumbled Keith, dimly aware that he had not made any sense, but hoping that Raul would believe that he had intended to say what he said.

"Yeah, I suppose so," Raul nodded, in frowning agreement.

Keith, one eye barely open, slowly picked up his towel and shaving kit and shuffled toward the bathroom. "Man!" Raul said, accompanying him, "on the street, my nickname was Lightnin', because I moved so slow, but compared to you now, I was supersonic!"

Keith, standing at a basin, said "Mmf," his mouth being full of toothbrush.

"They said we'd have cleaning detail this morning. Do you suppose that means latrines?" Raul asked.

Keith spat out slowly before answering, maintaining his even breathing, as he returned the slightly opened eyelid to the shut position. "Any ate," he mumbled incomprehensibly, and groped his way back to the bedroom.

"Wow, twenty-eight!" said Raul, tagging along.

When they reached the room, Ray was down from the top bunk and already in shirt and pants. "He says we're going to have to clean twenty-eight latrines this morning!" Raul exclaimed.

"You dumb greaseball! Can't you tell whitey's jivin' you? He's *laughin'* at you, man!"

"I wasn't laughing at him," Keith said, giving up sleep now, as a lost cause. "Truth is, I didn't hear a word he said."

"You calling me a liar?" Ray said menacingly.

"Take it any way you like," Keith said calmly, but wide awake.

"Come on, you guys," said Raul hastily, "we're going to be late for breakfast."

That morning, it turned out they did not clean latrines; they worked on the deep fat fryer, a much harder job. And that afternoon, they had their introduction to "Walking in the Light." In one of the classrooms, there were eleven chairs in a circle, three of them occupied by Hector, Charles and Don, the three group leaders, the rest of them by the men in Genesis. For the benefit of the newcomers, Hector explained what they would be doing. "There's a scripture in the first epistle of John that I want to read to you," and he read them I John 1:5-7, from the Revised Standard Version:

> This is the message we have heard from him
>   and proclaim to you,
> That God is light, and in him is no dark-
>   ness at all.
> If we say we have fellowship with him
>   while we walk in darkness,

We lie and do not live according to the
    truth;
But if we walk in the light, as he is in
    the light,
We have fellowship with one another,
And the blood of Jesus His Son cleanses
    us from all sin.

Hector went to the blackboard and wrote
vertically the word LIGHT. "One of the things
you're going to be learning at Teen Challenge,"
he said, turning around, "is how to walk in the
light with one another, just like that scripture
says. You're going to learn to be open and honest
with one another, just the way those first disciples
were. You'll do this in the groups you're assigned
to, working out the intra-family relationships you
may never have had. By God's grace and with the
guidance of his Holy Spirit, not only is it possible
to live like those early disciples, but it will be the
springboard that will launch you into a whole new
relationship — with God, and with everyone else
around you."

He paused, to let the point sink in. "And the
key is your willingness to be open and honest.
Possibly for the first time in your life, you're
going to learn what it is to be completely honest
with another individual. And you are also going
to learn that you can trust the Spirit of God in
another person, and that, in Him, it is safe to be
vulnerable. You're going to learn that correction
is not rejection, but love, although sometimes it
can be tough love, and that it is not annihilation
to be wrong. Jesus *came* for wrong ones, not for

the righteous!'' And he stopped, slightly abashed at his enthusiasm.

Turning back to the blackboard, he said, "*Light*, the way we use the word here, stands for" — and he wrote out the words as he spoke — "Living In Group Harmony through Truth. That's going to come to mean a great deal to you in the coming months.''

He came back to the circle and sat down. "Normally, the real emphasis on light wouldn't come until you get up to Camp Champion, but the three of us have gotten the distinct feeling that some of you are walking around in darkness and need to get some things into the light. So here we are. Let's pray,'' and he lowered his head, as did most of the others. "Lord, we turn this time over to you and ask that you will bring into the light whatever you want brought out, and that you will guide us by your Spirit into the ways of truth. We pray that you will bless us with an abundance of your gifts of wisdom, knowledge and discernment. We ask you to teach us that we can trust you operating in and through one another, and give us open and teachable hearts. And let anything that is not of you fall back to ashes and dust. We ask these things in your name, amen.'' And there were a few murmured amens.

"Now,'' said Hector, looking around the circle. "Who's got anything they feel needs to be brought up?'' No one said a word, or moved. "No problems, no hassles, nothing?'' A couple of men shifted slightly in their chairs, otherwise silence.

"Okay, who's having a problem in their room, with a roommate?" Raul gave a start, amazed, and looked to Keith and Ray, to see if they would say anything, but they both stared straight ahead, as if they had not heard what had just been said.

As Hector had spoken, Don noticed Raul's reaction. "Raul, what about it?" he queried. "Who's been hassling who?"

"Who, me?" said Raul, acting surprised. "I'm not hassling anybody. I'm as happy as a — "

"What about Ray and Keith," Charles said, interrupting him, "they happy with one another?"

"Why, sure!" Raul said emphatically.

"Oh, come off it!" snapped the feisty little Italian named Polo. "We practically had World War III out there on the basketball court yesterday afternoon!"

There was shocked silence at this flagrant transgression of the unwritten code of both street and stir: thou shalt not rat. Hector picked up on it immediately: "Listen, you guys, this is not jail, and we're not hacks. All we want to do is help you see who you are and how you affect other people, because when you see it, you'll have a better idea of how much you need God, and then you can really get some help. So relax: we're not going to be meting out any punishment or holding anything against you. This is the place where it's safe to be wrong, remember? Now be honest!"

There was still no response, but the guys in the circle began to relax. "Okay, Keith, what happened out there?"

"Nothing," he replied. "We went up for a

rebound, and I caught an elbow, that's all," and he shrugged, as if he couldn't understand what everyone was making such a big deal over.

"Ray?" Charles turned to him for corroboration.

"It's like he said, Cap. We went up, and I just sort of tapped him. Accidentally, you understand," and he also smiled, as if he, too, were mystified at all the fuss.

"What did he say?" Don persisted.

"Oh, he complained a little about it, as if it weren't an accident. But I figured that was on account of he —"

"It was no accident," Keith cut in, quietly. Ray flashed him a warning look, but Keith ignored it. "He gave me a shot as soon as I went up for a rebound. He doesn't care much for white people, I've gathered," Keith added, deciding that it might as well all come out.

"How about it, Ray?" asked Charles. "You got something against us white folks?"

"Why, no," Ray said, sounding casual. "Some of my best friends are white." He laughed, but only one or two joined with him.

Now everyone was holding his breath. Charles was about to speak, but Hector, sitting next to him, put a hand on his arm, and then whispered something to him. Charles nodded, and seemingly out of the blue, Hector turned to Larry and asked him, "Larry, who was the best player out there?" Everyone, including Larry, was taken off guard by this seemingly unrelated query.

"Uh, Keith was. It looked like he'd played

71

before. You know, on a team, or something. But after it happened, he sat out."

"And then who was the best player?"

"Well, I guess Ray was."

"At least he talked the best game," Polo cracked. Ray shot a murderous glance in his direction, but Polo was unfazed.

"You know," said Hector, "this really doesn't have anything to do with skin color. What we've got here is one of the oldest sins in the book: plain old jealousy." There was a murmur of surprise and recognition in the group. "Do you see that, Ray?"

"No way, man! I don't mean to be disrespectful, but somebody'd have to be outa their tree, to think he'd have anything I'd be jealous of!"

"Well," Hector said patiently, "you're usually number one man in any crowd you happen to be in, aren't you?"

"Well, sure," Ray laughed, and this time everyone joined in.

"But suddenly you weren't number one under the boards, is that right?"

"All depends on how you look at it," Ray said smoothly. "He's not bad for a rich boy. 'Course, he doesn't understand how we play street ball."

"I'm going to ask you again," said Charles. "Have you got something against white folks? Especially rich ones?"

"Nothin', Cap," said Ray, holding his hands out, palms up, "nothin' at all."

Now it was Hector who spoke.

"Ray, you come from Harlem?"

"Sure. Don't just about everyone in this town, with a sunburn like mine?" and he enjoyed the laughter that brought.

"What about your folks — they come from Harlem, too?"

"My mother came from Carolina," he said, suddenly guarded in his speech.

"What about your father?"

"The same."

"How'd your father support the family?"

"He didn't. He split before I was born." Ray's voice was barely audible now. It was obvious that these were things he had not thought of for a long time, out of choice, and would not have volunteered. But Hector was patient, and the rest of the group was sympathetic in their silence.

"How'd your mother support you?" Hector asked.

"She cleaned house."

"Go on," Hector encouraged him.

"Each day, she would go to a different Miss Anne's house," Ray recalled, acid edging his words. "She'd work all day long: 'Clean the oven, Haddie,' or 'You didn't do a good enough job in the master bathroom, Haddie; go do it over.' She'd come home exhausted, and I'd try to do something for her. I was only seven, eight, but I could make soup and a cup of hot tea for her. Then on Sundays, she wouldn't sleep in and get some rest; no, she took me and my older brother, when he was home, to church. And she'd sit there and listen to that Reverend Lowdown tell how much Jesus loved us and was preparing a

73

place for us in heaven, and all that — uh, stuff."

"How'd you come to Harlem?"

"It finally got so my mother couldn't do like she used to. She'd gotten older, and so had I — my brother had split by then — and those rich Miss Annes with the two new cars and the big houses wouldn't give her more than 35 cents an hour. They all knew one another, and they agreed together that they wouldn't 'spoil' Haddie by giving her a raise. So one day those rich white ladies had no one to come clean their big houses. Mama had a sister in Harlem, and on we came. But when we got here, the only work she could find was cleaning. She could have gone on welfare, but she was too proud for that. This time, it was apartments — nice, luxury apartments on the upper East side. With nice, luxury Miss Annes telling her, 'Clean the oven, Haddie,' and 'You didn't do a good job on the master bathroom, Haddie; go do it again.'"

He stopped, and there was a long silence. Finally, Hector spoke: "Was she bitter about what she was doing, Ray?"

"No, man, she wasn't. She shoulda been, but she'd gotten too big a dose of your so-called Christianity. She's accepted it as her lot in life. But not me, not old Razor Daniels. I got another way of lookin' at things," and he sat back, tapping the tips of his fingers together, his cool restored.

"You love your mother very much, don't you?" said Hector quietly.

"Well, sure!" exclaimed Ray, "what kind of a question is that? Don't you?"

Hector nodded without directly answering.

"Did it ever occur to you that you might be waging a one-man war on her behalf? That you're projecting your own pride on her, and that if she could, she would just as soon call a halt to your war?"

"Hey, listen!" shot back Ray, "there's eight guys in this circle! How come you're spending so much time on me?"

"It could be the Lord," Charles suggested. "It could be that He's trying to help you see why you do the things you do. And why you need Him. You do, you know, but you're not going to see it all at once. Just think about the things that have been said to you." The conversation shifted then, to Larry, and before long, it was over.

That night, as the three were getting ready for bed, Raul said, "Man, that light session was something else! I had the feeling like — I don't know, that God was there, watching. I never felt anything like it." No one said anything. "And sometimes it seemed like the group leaders could see right inside you." Ray glared at him. "I didn't mean you personally," Raul hastened to add, "I meant me, Larry, anyone."

"It really gives a person something to think about," Keith mused, partly to get Raul off the hook. But only partly.

"Well, you can think about it all you like," Ray said sarcastically. "I'm not gonna waste my time on it." Placing his hands on the edge of the upper bunk, with just his arms he raised himself up on it, then turned back for a parting shot: "You can play your little group games, if you want to, but nobody's getting to old Razor. Nobody!" And he rolled over and faced the wall.

7

Choosing

The next two weeks passed swiftly and uneventfully. Polo and Larry left for Camp Champion, and two new young men came into Genesis, to take their place. For Raul, it was a new world. Everyone was friendly, and there were others in the program with backgrounds almost identical to his own. The enthusiasm with which he initially greeted each day gradually began to extend longer and longer, until he was grinning most of the time. For him, life had become almost like one of those musical comedies he occasionally watched on the late show. Like Fred Astaire and Gene Kelly in Navy boot camp, dancing as they cleaned the barracks, for Raul, even cleaning the latrines seemed to bring him joy.

The staff, of course, noticed the change and encouraged him at every opportunity. In fact, it was one of the first things that Joe mentioned to Randy, when Randy pulled in from Camp Champion and asked him how things were going.

"I've seen guys change fast," Joe said, "but this guy Castenada is almost unbelievable! He came up to me at lunch yesterday, to try to wheedle out of me what Genesis' weekend activity would be, and if I'd told him that it was to dig up the street out in front for Con Ed, he would have been delighted!"

Hector dropped into Joe's office just at that moment and smiled. "You must be talking about Raul," he said. "Yeah, he's something else, all right. And wait till he accepts the Lord; he'll be in orbit! Don says he's going faster through the *New Look at Life* book than any of the others. There's no question that he's giving 100%." Hector paused. "And he's got guts, too. He's beginning to stand up to Ray. Which makes Ray furious, of course. The Rays in this world need the Rauls — the little guys they can always put down — because they have to have that constant confirmation of their innate superiority. Take away their ego-prop, and they're in trouble."

"Unfortunately," said Joe, "the opposite is also true: the Rauls in this world often seem to have some sick need for the Rays — the older brother, the unattainable role model, the perfection that hopefully rubs off a little on them, when their presence is tolerated. Raul is a follower; he's been one all his life, and still is. The encouraging thing is, he's following Keith, rather than Ray. And the ways things are going, it shouldn't be too long before he's following Jesus, instead of Keith."

"Sounds good," Randy said to Joe. "Speaking of Keith, how's he doing?"

"Something of a spaceman, I'm afraid," Joe replied. "I've seen him trip out a few times. All of a sudden his eyes glaze over, and you get the feeling, he's checked out. Like he's visiting another planet."

"Funny you should say that," Hector smiled, "because you know who his favorite author is? Tolkien. Sure, I know all the kids are into Tolkien these days, the way they were into Vonnegut in my day. But with him, it's different. He devours the stuff. According to Don, he's also read everything that Heinlein and Bradbury have written, and half a dozen other guys I've never heard of. And Charles says he's seen 'Star Wars' seven times. That's where it is, for him."

"But when he's 'in residence', as it were, he's more or less with it," Joe said. "In sports, in group activities, light sessions, meals — he's got a nice spirit."

"Good. Let's keep him in reality as much as possible, then. Pass the word: anyone who sees him spacing out, call him on it. We're not going to be able to reach him, unless he's standing on solid ground." Randy thought for a moment. "What about the other one that came in at the same time, Ray Daniels?"

Neither Joe nor Hector said anything. Finally Hector spoke. "He talks a good game — a perfect game, in fact; except the day after he got here, when he opened up a little in a light session. Since then, not a crack. And that's what it is with him: a game. He plays all the right cards, but I get a funny feeling he's dealing from the bottom of the deck."

79

"Remember what I said, when he was inducted?" Joe said. "He's Mr. Cool. But he and Keith are still sandpaper and file. It shouldn't be too long before something happens that will give us the handle."

Hector got what he needed from Joe and left, and Randy told Joe he had a special reason for asking about Ray, Raul and Keith. "We can take three more at the Camp. Shekinah's full up, but Alpha just sent two to the Farm, and we had to put one guy out — Andrew Bennett."

Joe shook his head. "I was hoping he was going to make it. I liked that big guy."

"I did, too," Randy agreed. "But he wouldn't be wrong. Every time someone tried to tell him something, he had an answer for them. You know, either explaining why he wasn't wrong, or pointing out where the person who was speaking to him, was himself wrong. Even when the whole group would try to show him, he'd fight them. Or seem to accept it, and then a day later show that he hadn't accepted it at all. Finally, he was just plain hostile. So the group recommended that he be put out. I told him that until he made up his mind to get serious with God, and get his life together, he would have to stay out. He left last Wednesday, shaking the dust from his sandals."

"I think he'll be back," predicted Joe.

"I hope so. Having to be right is a pretty miserable place to live. I guess he's got to learn the hard way, that his problem isn't with the program or the place or the people. It's with himself."

"Well, when he comes back," Joe said optimistically, "he'll be needy and really looking for help, and he'll make up for lost time."

"*If* he comes back," Randy corrected him. "He's got a lot of pride; I don't know if he could ever bring himself to be that wrong."

Joe took Bennett's file out, to up-date it. "Oh, he'll run on hate for a while, but eventually that will get kind of old, to himself and everyone else, and all that'll be left will be self-pity. In due time, he'll get a bellyful of that, and then he'll be able to see it."

"Like I said," concluded Randy, less optimistic, "I hope so." He brightened up. "But look: what about these three openings?"

"Like you heard," Joe smiled, "Raul and Keith are ready right now. Ray — well, frankly, I doubt that he'll ever be ready, unless something happens. And it's more likely to happen up there than down here. I'd say, take him, too."

"Good. Tell them they're coming up Friday. And be sure to tell Don Richmond, so he can take them through the end of *A New Look at Life.*" Randy got up to leave, when the phone rang. Joe answered it, and then held up his hand for Randy to wait. "It's Matt Rocco," he said, with his hand over the receiver, "he's calling about Keith." Randy waited, while Joe finished the call. "Hey, that's great... You've got to be kidding.... Oh, praise God! Randy's right here; I'll tell him .... Okay, Matt; God bless," and he hung up. up.

Joe looked up at Randy. "You're not going to

81

believe this!'' he said, grinning and shaking his head.

The following morning, Raul was unusually silent, as they got dressed, and Keith blissfully drifted back from the bathroom and into his clothes in a state of heavenly rest. It wasn't until he had floated down the stairs and was on his way out the door, that he became aware of a persistent nagging thought: it was too quiet. Raul should have made at least a dozen observations by now that would have required token nerms. (Keith had resorted to answering Raul by saying ''nerm'' under his breath at the appropriate interval, and nodding, and this seemed to satisfy Raul.)

Keith pried both eyes open, squinted at the July sunlight, and studied his friend. Raul didn't seem unhappy; in fact, he was wearing a sort of canary-eating grin. Keith returned his lids to the semi-shut navigating position, and erased the blackboard of his mind.

And now Raul spoke. ''Can you believe we've been here more than two weeks already?''

''Nerm.''

They entered 444 on their way to the dining hall for breakfast. ''There's where we sat, the three of us, waiting for our interviews.'' He looked over at Keith, who nodded and said, ''Nerm.''

''And remember the first time we came in this dining hall? Man, it seems like it was another century!''

''Long ago, in a galaxy far, far away . . .'' Keith recited, from the opening of ''Star Wars''.

Raul looked at him quizzically. "It's hard, sometimes, to tell which reality is the real one," Keith murmured, by way of explanation.

Ray had preceded them, and was sitting by himself, and Keith made a point of joining him, though a couple of the other guys had waved to him. If Ray appreciated their company, he gave no indication, answering a couple of attempts at conversation with little more than a grunt. Just then, Charles came by their table and said, "Got some good news for you guys; you'll be going to Camp Champion tomorrow."

"Wow! That really settles it!" Raul said, getting up from the table. "I'll see you guys in chapel; there's a little matter I got to take care of first." And he left his eggs and muffins almost untouched.

"Where you going?" called Charles after him.

"Just to chapel," Raul smiled, and went out the door.

Charles shrugged and turned back to the others. "That man really *is* getting turned on! Actually," he continued to Ray and Keith, "the whole group is going up tomorrow afternoon, as their weekend activity, but you three will be staying." He started to leave, then turned back. "Oh, and Keith: Mr. Larson wants to see you in his office after chapel."

"I wonder what I've done now?" Keith muttered, after Charles had left. When he and Ray joined the others in the chapel, there was Raul in the front row, his head bowed, his lips moving slightly. Keith shook his head, and took a seat about half-way down, while Ray sat in the back.

The chapel service seemed interminable, and Keith was too agitated to relax. Finally, the time came when Sandy, the office manager said, "Mr. Larson will see you now."

As he came in, Randy said, "Sit down; I've got some news for you. And it's good news, so you can stop running down your sin list." Keith cocked his head. "We've heard from Mr. Rocco: Mr. Henderson is out of danger; he's going to be fine." Randy smiled at Keith whose face was expressionless. Then his eyes brimmed, and that said it all.

"And that's not all," Randy said. "Mr. Henderson refuses to press charges, and Mr. Rocco has talked to the judge in charge of your case. He knows Teen Challenge, and he is prepared to postpone your trial date for four months to see how you do. Mr. Rocco says that there's a good chance he will give you a suspended sentence if you stay in the program, provided that you do well in it. I am to send the judge a monthly written report on you." Randy stopped, and Keith just sat there, speechless.

"There's one more thing you ought to know. Mr. Rocco says that Mr. Henderson has been praying for you — every day, since he regained consciousness. His first prayer was one thanking God that you were all right." Keith looked up at him, and then broke down and sobbed uncontrollably.

That afternoon, in Don Richmond's class, Raul, Keith and Ray completed the last lesson in *A New Look at Life*. Its title: The Big Choice. In previous lessons, they had looked at the things in their lives that had prevented them from hearing God speak to them, seen what happened to those lives when they had lived for themselves or tried to make it on their own, and then considered the Bible in terms of it being the Manufacturer's handbook. They had learned that God had a definite plan for each of their lives, and that He gave laws as guides to help us enjoy life. They had seen the penalty for breaking God's laws, and that Jesus had come to pay the penalty for them, if they were sorry for what they had done and asked God to forgive them. And they learned that, just as Jesus Himself was resurrected, He would lift them out of a living death of unconfessed sin. There was no need to spend the rest of eternity in a hell that would be far worse than the worst of the ones they were already living in; there *was* a way out. The way was faith in a living, risen Jesus Christ.

To have the new life that God offered, they must give up one more thing: control of their own lives. From now on, He had to be the leader; they, the followers.

And so they came to that final lesson. They were to circle one of the following four choices:

1. Yes, I want to become a Christian.

2. No, I'm not ready to become a Christian.

3. I'm not sure if I am a Christian.

4. I already am a Christian.

Ray promptly circled #1. Raul circled #4, adding in a parenthetical note, (*I gave my heart to the Lord in chapel this morning*).

And Keith, after long reflection, circled #2.

8

Smores

Camp Champion is a gift straight from God. Three hundred and eighty acres of secluded woodland in the lower Catskill Mountains, it is a two-hour drive north from New York City, and about half an hour north of where Interstate 84 crosses the Pennsylvania/New York border. In the middle of the property is a sixty-acre lake, eighteen cabins for summer campers, three bathhouses, a recreation hall, a dining hall, and a beautiful rustic chapel overlooking a rolling green lawn, well cared for by resident manager, Miller Fagley.

About four years ago, it had become increasingly apparent to us that we had to find a place outside the ghetto environment of 416 Clinton for our induction center, a place where the guys in our program could have a chance to sink their roots into the Christian life and put down a strong tap-root of tested faith. The Farm, of course, provided this for the last eight months of the Teen Challenge program, but those first four months were crucial, and the lure of the street was so strong where we were, that students were being pulled away before they had a chance to put down roots.

So we started praying for a farm or a camp — a place that would be completely the opposite of the concrete and glass and steel and traffic that most of our young men grew up in. Exactly what and where, we left up to the Lord, who knew our needs, present and future, far better than we did. But we imagined it would be a place of softness and peace, where the natural beauty of His creation would minister to the spirits of the fellows in the program, as much as anything we could say to them, or do for them. As for 416, we would keep it going as a crisis center, a place where we could bring addicts whom we had reached on the streets, and where they could dry out or go through detox for a week or so. It would also be a place where people could come with other severe problems, like the boy who stumbled in recently, having just slashed his wrists. But the four-month Light program, we would move to wherever the Lord provided.

In my heart, I felt sure that the Lord *would* provide just such a place. And just about that time — in fact, shortly after we had started praying — an extraordinary thing happened that has never happened before or since, in our ministry: the Lord started sending in more money than we needed. Normally, or rather, almost predictably, we receive just enough money to pay our monthly bills, and if an emergency arises, just enough more somehow comes in to cover it. It has always been thus with Teen Challenge; it seems to be God's way of keeping us ever mindful of our abiding need of His grace and mercy, and of keeping us out of control of His program. Indeed, it seems to be a pattern He first established with the Israelites wandering in the wilderness: each day the cloud would show them the way, the fire would keep them by night, and in the morning there would always be enough fresh manna for that day's needs.

But now, suddenly, that pattern was broken. I took it as an encouragement and instructed our business manager to do likewise, and not spend the extra funds on justifiable but inessential expenditures, but let them accumulate. And accumulate they did — $25,000, then $50,000, then $75,000! I began to get uneasy. There were certain divisions of our work that were having financial struggles, and there was a great temptation to bail them out. But I still sensed that God had a special purpose in mind, and so I waited — and grew increasingly uneasy.

Then one day, I got a call from California, from Jim Vaus. Jim had been saved at a Billy Graham Crusade in Los Angeles, in 1952. His conversion had made quite a stir at the time, because Jim had been Mickey Cohen's wiretapper and the first known member of the Cosa Nostra to accept Jesus Christ as his Lord and Savior. He had subsequently written several books and been called by God to New York, to work with street gangs. Indeed, he preceded David in this mission field. As an extension of his street ministry, and with the financial help of George Champion (David Rockefeller's predecessor at Chase

Manhattan Bank), he founded Camp Champion. Designing it to provide inner city youngsters with a chance to go to a first-class summer camp, they made it one of the most beautiful camps in the northeastern United States.

But that was many years ago, and now, as he explained to me on the phone, Jim was being led in another direction, and his organization wanted to find another Christian organization to take over the camp. As I listened, I said to myself, Lord, that can't be you! Camp Champion is so much more than we had in mind, or could even consider as a possibility! But — I went to see it.

And it blew out all my circuits! Being the sort of person I am, I bottled up all my emotions, refusing to let myself get excited about it. Instead, I kept reminding myself of all the big properties that had become millstones and even nooses around the necks of growing Christian works. And yet, my heart noted, the property was immaculate! Some camps are so run down, they are practically slums in the woods; you might send your kids there, but you would never want to go there yourself. Not Camp Champion; it had everything — vehicles, bedding, boats, life-jackets, and even a snowmobile! And it was ready; the cabins were winterized — we could be moved in and be operating in twenty-four hours.

There was a hitch, of course. The board of Jim's organization did not know very much about Teen Challenge. About all they did know was that it was run by Pentecostals, and of course everyone knew that Pentecostals were unstable and just ran on their emotions [*sic!*], so we had to demonstrate to them our fiscal and administrative responsibility. So *that* was God's reason for letting us accumulate all that capital!

By now, my heart had again won out, and I was emotionally committed to the prospect; in fact, I was dying for it to happen! But — we were still short of the sum required for the downpayment. Way short. About $19,000 short. And then one day, a few weeks later, while I was down in Texas conferring with David, I got a phone call from my wife Cindy. "I have some news," she said.

"Good or bad?"

"Well, you'd better sit down."

"Oh, no, what is it?" I said, standing up.

"We've just gotten a check for $19,900!"

"Hallelujah!"

And that's how Camp Champion became a part of Teen Challenge. I was euphoric, but then the Lord sat me down and showed me a few things. It was because of our obedience that He was able to bless us. He had given us an assignment, to see how well we carried it out. It happened to be a tough assignment: we were to reach out to street people whom others had written off, in the worst ghettos in New York, and perhaps the world. When we began, it was so bad that the precinct station down the street from us was nicknamed "Fort Apache". We were to live with these people, eat with them, walk with them — and pray with them. We were to meet these people where *they* were at, and we were to show them — not by what we said or did, but by who we were, inside — that there was another way, that they, too, could have Him inside.

We did it to the best of our ability, staying up all night with addicts kicking heroin cold turkey, talking and listening for hours, often to be rejected in the end, going into places and situations that even the police were wary of, working twelve, sixteen, eighteen hours a day for little more than room and board. And we did it cheerfully. Sure, we blew it many times, but we tried our best to stay out of self and in Christ, and to be led by His Spirit. And as we worked, we came to know ourselves, and to know just how true it was that there was no good thing in us, save Christ, and if anything good came out of us, that was His doing, not ours, and sheer grace that enabled us to do it at all. We could not take credit for anything.

What God was showing me that morning was that, in His mercy, He was honoring our obedience. He also showed me that our assignment followed a pattern established by His Son. Jesus never shrank from going into the slums to reach the poor. He ate with harlots and thieves, publicans and sinners. He shared their lot and was accused of being a winebibber and worse, because of the company He kept. But He also took His disciples aside with Him, so that He could teach them and show them a new way of living.

Our assignment was to reach the poor (in spirit, as well as in possessions), and then to take them aside and show them the same new way.

It was about two in the afternoon, when the van loaded with Genesis group pulled up with

Hector at the wheel. As they piled out, craning their heads up to look at the lofty fir trees like tourists to Manhattan looking at the skyscrapers, I asked Randy, who was standing with me on the verandah of the admin building, what he was going to do with them. "Would you believe that I'm going to take them on a nature hike? Hector talked me into it. But wait till he sees what we'll organize for him, when one of our groups from here goes down to Brooklyn for a visit!" I laughed, as Randy went down to talk to Hector and tell the group where they would be spending the night. In the morning, Keith, Ray and Raul would be joining Alpha group, and the rest would be returning to Brooklyn. This was to be their last outing as a group.

They went to stow their gear, and a half-hour later, they were reassembled, and Randy was giving them their marching orders. "We'll go in single file," he was telling them, "and we'll go quietly, because there's a family of deer that sometimes feeds in the late afternoon on the other side of a ridge not far from here. Keep it closed up, so you'll be able to hear what I have to say, without my having to shout." And without saying anything more, he started off, the others scrambling to get in line behind him.

Despite Randy's admonition, the group was boisterous, to say the least, wisecracking and poking one another. "Hey, Tony!" a young Puerto Rican named Carlos called to the back of the column, "run up to the front, and ask Mr. Larson if he wants us to count cadence, like in those old John Wayne movies."

"Why don't *you* run up there," Tony retorted,

"you're the one who's good at running — especially running off at the mouth!" And everyone laughed. "Yeah," someone else said, "don't tell Carlos to count anything; he'll have to take his shoes off and use his toes to get it to come out right." More guffaws.

"Hey! Here's a rabbit track!" exclaimed a young black boy named Thomas, who had never been off the island of Manhattan in his life, pointing to the ground in front of him, his mouth open in awe. Immediately, everyone stopped and crowded around him, staring at the ground he indicated, which looked exactly like all the other ground around them.

"That ain't no rabbit track!" Tony scoffed, "is it, Mr. Larson? You ding-a-ling," he exclaimed, cuffing Thomas playfully, "you wouldn't know a rabbit track, if you was to fall into one!"

"Maybe you'd better leave the nature pointers to me," Randy chuckled, and they continued on their way. He led them over a couple of fairly steep hills to wind them down a bit, and after a while they lapsed into silence, concentrating on the terrain directly in front of them. Randy was able to show them a skin that was recently shed by a snake, a hawk's nest, and a rabbit warren, which even had a rabbit scamper away from it.

"Wow!" said Thomas. "Did you see that? That was a rabbit! That's the closest I've ever been to a real live rabbit, except one time when I rented myself out for a quarter at the Central Park Children's Zoo!"

"You did what?" asked Hector, trying not to laugh.

"At that zoo," explained Thomas, surprised at the question, "you had to have a kid with you, in order to get in, and grown-up couples would come by and want to go in, so for a quarter, I would be their kid."

"Oh," said Hector, biting his lip.

Just then, Randy raised his hand, signalling for everyone to be still. "If the deer are here," he whispered, "they'll be just over that ridge there," and he pointed towards a long, low hill that seemed almost irridescent in the late afternoon sun. "But we'll have to make a lot less noise than the IRT, if we're going to see them." And he stood perfectly still, listening. Everyone else did likewise. There were crickets and insects, and a few distant songbirds, but for all that, it was remarkably quiet, almost as if something on the other side of the ridge was listening, too.

Slowly, almost at a creep, Randy led them forward, signalling for them to fan out, in a rough line abreast. Eyes wide, ears straining to hear the slightest sound, they approached the rim of the ridge. Suddenly, a huge, dark-winged shape launched itself from one of the trees in front of them, and swooped low over them and out of sight farther down the ridge. *"Yeow!"* burst out Ray, at whom it had seemed at first to be flying. *"What was that?"*

"Wild turkey," said Randy. "Come on!" he called and waved everyone forward, as he ran for the top of the ridge. But when they got there, there was nothing to be seen.

A couple of the guys were put out with Ray and started to say something to him, but Randy said, "Look, it could have happened to anyone. But the good thing about this place is that they'll be back. We might even see them this evening, down by the lake. Now come on, let's see if we can find some traces," and he motioned to them to spread out and look on the ground.

Before long, he called them to him again. "Here," he said, pointing to the ground, "those are deer droppings. And they're fresh, from the look of them. Which means that they *were* here. Well, if you don't see them this weekend, you will when you transfer up here." And he led them back to camp.

There was a surprise waiting for them, when they returned. For supper, Jose, the camp cook, had prepared a cookout for them. With long sticks, they would be roasting hotdogs over a campfire, and for dessert an added surprise: smores.

"What are smores?" Raul asked.

"Well," said Randy, "let's just say that they're so good that the first thing you say when you taste one is, 'Can I have s'more?' " There were a number of groans. Hector passed out long sticks for them to put their hotdogs on, and soon they were bringing them to a sizzle, putting them in buns, and loading them with ketchup, mustard, chopped onions and relish. When it came time for dessert, Norman Miller appeared carrying a tray laden with marshmallows, graham crackers and chocolate bars. Norman was a fast-talking, gregarious black from the streets of Chicago, who had been through the program himself the year before, and who was interning for a year before going on to Bible school.

Possessed of a gentle but right-on sense of humor, he was one of Alpha's group leaders, and the Camp's resident expert on smores.

"I hope you saved your sticks," he said, "or can retrieve them. Because I am about to demonstrate the culinary art of smore-making. Observe," he said, holding up a marshmallow between thumb and forefinger, "this is a marshmallow." A couple of guys cheered this observation, and the rest laughed.

"It is placed on the stick, like so," Norman continued, his aplomb intact, "and one holds it over the coals like so." He lowered it to perhaps six inches from a still-glowing area. "Now there are two things that are important here: patience and concentration. Patience, because if you lose patience, you'll move the marshmallow too close, and it will catch fire and char itself black, instead of toasting to the ideal golden brown that is desired. And you need concentration, because, if you're not careful, the inside of the marshmallow will begin to melt, and it will slide right off the end of your —." He was cut off by a howl of laughter, as his marshmallow plopped onto the coals and was quickly consumed.

Scandalized, Norman tried again, this time with more success. Taking two graham crackers, he put a piece of a chocolate bar on one, the toasted marshmallow on the other one and closed them into a sandwich, in which the hot marshmallow just melted the chocolate. "*Deewiphus!*" he marveled, his mouth full of smore. Soon the others were gathered around, and clusters of marshmallows were bobbing over the

97

coals, with some occasionally charring and others occasionally plopping in, to everyone's amusement.

It was getting darker out, but the coals made a cheery glow, and after the last smore was devoured, the guys put some wood on the fire and sat around, learning songs young people had sung around campfires for at least half a century.

Shortly before it got to be time for bed, Keith, who had been down to the lake, came back and whispered for Raul and Ray to come with him, telling them to be quiet. He led them down to the water's edge, where they had an unobstructed view of the lake. There was a night mist rising from the water in several places, but where it was clear, the full moon was perfectly reflected on a mirror-smooth surface. They stood there for a moment, astonished by the hushed beauty of what they saw. "Over there," Keith barely whispered and pointed to an outcropping of land, less than a hundred feet from where they stood. There, silhouetted in the moonlight, were three dark forms, their heads down, drinking at the edge of the lake.

Raul slowly smiled, but Ray's eyes widened. "They're *animals*!" he whispered, his voice trembling.

"That's right," Keith whispered calmly, trying to steady him, "it must be the family of deer Mr. Larson told us about this afternoon." But it had no effect.

One of the deer raised his head and looked in their direction. "*He's seen us*!" hissed Ray. "Man, I'm gettin' outa here!" and he bolted back to the fire. The deer, startled, suddenly disappeared into the inky blackness of the woods. Keith and Raul went back to the fire, to share what they had seen.

"Oh, man!" Ray was telling the others, when they got there. "He was as big as a car, and when he saw us and was going to charge —"

Keith shook his head, chuckling. "He was more scared of you, than you were of him! No matter; they're gone now."

"They were beautiful," Raul said, awestruck, "the most beautiful things I've ever seen."

9

Where You Sit is Where You Stand

Dawn didn't break, Saturday morning; it sifted down through the limbs of oak and fir trees in glimmering hazy fragments. First it woke the birds, who opened their eyes and shook out their feathers, then greeted the morning with increasingly confident song. Soon the squirrels joined in, chattering away like housewives on a party line. The crickets, grasshoppers and insect life were next awakened, adding their resonance to the morning symphony. And finally it woke the members of Genesis, all save one or two who had been startled awake by the unfamiliar sound of the first early bird, while it was yet dark.

It had been decided to let them sleep in a bit, since this outing was a special treat for them, and because sleep is an important part of the initial healing process of someone who has been strung out on dope for a long time, as a number of the men in Genesis had been. So was a hearty breakfast, and that morning in the dining hall, they were served hot cereal, followed by eggs, bacon, toast, and all the milk they wanted. Maybe it was the fresh air, or being in the outdoors, or just the change in environment, that made them hungry, but there were big appetites that morning.

After breakfast, Keith, Ray and Raul said goodbye to the others who were headed back to Brooklyn, and went with Norman Miller. When they reached the cabin that Alpha group occupied, Norman introduced the new guys around. "Okay, you guys, this here is Keith Lawson, and Raul Castenada, and Ray Daniels. And now for the rogues' gallery: meet Stas Walinsky, the handsomest Pole in Alpha group. He is also the ugliest Pole, depending on how you look at him, since he's the only Pole. We have here Mr. James Turner, a prominent albeit diminutive member of my own race, who will be going to the Farm before too much longer, as will this fine albeit silent specimen of manhood Amos Brown. By way of contrast, here we have Jose Santiago, the size and ability of whose lip is rivaled only by that of Polo Ippolito, whose acquaintance I believe you have already made. You have also been formerly acquainted with Larry Zonas here, and now that the introductions are completed, I want everyone up on the softball field at ten o'clock."

Ray, Raul and Keith picked out empty bunks, stowed their gear, and went with the others up to the diamond. Standing there with Norman was Simon Beteta, the senior group leader of Alpha, plus Pete Rios, the senior group leader from Shekinah. The guys from Alpha joined the others from Shekinah, and listened as Simon spoke to them: "As you characters know, fostering a spirit of competition is not what this place is all about. But we think we're supposed to have a ballgame this morning, and you can't very well do that, unless you've got two teams. So we're going to divvy up the two groups. Try to remember that you're playing for the fun of it, and for the fellowship, and that the World Series is not going to be decided on the outcome." And with that, the staff separated them into two teams.

Simon asked the men on his team what positions they had played, and there was a lot of kidding around, a couple of them talking as if it were only a quirk of misfortune that the Yankees' scouts had somehow overlooked them. A couple of others said nothing, but their actions indicated that they considered anyone who could get excited at the prospect of hitting a ball with a stick as beneath contempt. Nevertheless, they were all soon in position, and as it turned out, Larry, Keith, Raul, Jose, and Polo were all on the same team.

It turned out to be quite a lively game, with more than a few surprises. Polo turned out to be almost as good at shortstop as the game he talked. He got three scratch singles by virtue of his speed, and he stole more bases than all the other players combined. Jose couldn't resist shouting from the bench, when Polo had slid into second, "Hey, man, just steal the bases; you don't have to shoplift them!" and both teams convulsed with laughter. Polo's biggest play of the morning was a grandstand, diving, over-the-shoulder catch — the only trouble being that, dazzled by sudden glory, he forgot about the runner on third who had tagged up and was streaking for home. Too late, he saw what was happening and threw the ball wildly — clean over the backstop, allowing another run.

Ray struck out once, swinging for a home run, and thereafter pretty much went through the motions. Raul drew walks twice — he seemed to have a gift for presenting a small strike zone — and each time he reached first, he was as delighted as if he had hit a home run. It didn't matter that both times he got put out, once by a pick-off and once in a run-down; he was irrepressible. "Hey, Keith, did you see that?" he exclaimed, returning to the bench. "I nearly stole second!"

Keith nodded and smiled, and then chuckled to himself. As it turned out, Keith hit the longest ball of the morning — a triple which scored the winning run. But it was something else he did which caught Simon's eye. Working behind the bench, as his team was taking its turn at bat, Keith tried to teach Larry the right stance to take in the batter's box, and how to meet a pitch and follow through.

When the game was over, they went down to the lake, to swim off the new dock that was there for the summer camp program. Each summer, some six hundred disadvantaged kids from New York City would come in four different groups for five days each. The first group would be arriving in a week, at which time the Light program would be moving into new quarters that were just being finished for it — two beautiful houses, set off in a completely separate area, with an activities building which they would share in common. The houses were first-class homes, set up to function as the center of each family unit, and made possible by gifts from Teen Challenge's supporters and generous grants from the Heyden Foundation and the Kresge Foundation.

With much shouting, there was a volley of cannonballs, as one form after another, black, brown and white, leaped off the dock, eyes tightly shut, nose tightly pinched. When the multiple explosions and their resulting spray subsided, Keith, Ray, and one or two others were left standing on the dock. "You going in?" Keith said to Ray.

"In my time, man, in my time."

Keith shrugged and stepped to the edge of the dock. Taking a couple of rapid, deep breaths, he curled his toes over the edge of the dock and crouched, then uncoiled and sprang out in a flat, racer's dive. But instead of breaking into a sprint, he coasted, gazing at the greenish-brown forms on the bottom as they slowly passed beneath him. He drifted until all his momentum was expended, then, without raising his head from the water, took a single breaststroke and glided some more. Finally, he rolled over and gazed at the blue sky and the white cumulus clouds that drifted overhead. After a while, he turned and headed back towards the rest, lazily reaching out in long, graceful strokes that were in marked contrast with the choppy, thrashing

105

motions of most of the other swimmers. When he got back in their midst, he noticed that Ray was standing only waist deep in the water, and he started to say something, but at that moment was pulled down from behind by Raul, playing shark.

After half an hour or so, Norman waved them in, and twenty minutes later, everyone was eating peanut butter and jelly sandwiches and potato salad, with fruit cocktail for dessert. "There'll be an hour's quiet time, and then we've got a job that needs doing. You can walk, sleep, read, or do nothing at all. But no talking," Norman said, and when the meal was finished and the dining hall cleared, they fanned out, each going his own way. Raul went for a walk around the lake, a Bible in his hand. Ray went back to the cabin and lay down on his bunk. Keith also went down to the lake. After a bit, he found what he was looking for: a large, flat, warm expanse of rock, right by the water's edge. He lay down on his back, looking up at the sky, and listening to the water lapping softly against the rock.

The next morning, there was a chapel service, and I was to give the sermon. As we sang some of the old choruses that were now becoming familiar to the most recent arrivals, I looked out over the congregation and noted where they were sitting. They were still fairly scattered, as we didn't make them sit together in church, and it was interesting to note where the different individuals sat. Ray, for instance, was in the back, in the very last pew. Keith was about half-way forward, and Raul was right up front.

I smiled: long ago, I had observed that where a man sat in chapel was a fairly accurate indicator of where he stood with the Lord. And then I chuckled to myself: was this a new interpretation of that verse in Psalm 129: "Thou knowest my downsitting and my uprising"? But I had also observed what I called the Holy Spirit push, which seemed to propel a person forward, the more yielded to Christ his heart became. And I remembered then, Randy's mentioning that at the first chapel service which they had attended, all three of them sat in the back row.

I didn't know exactly what I was going to preach on. But then I seldom did, relying instead on the Holy Spirit giving me a Scripture verse, or calling to mind an incident on which to begin. But this morning, there was nothing. Lord? I prayed as I got to my feet. I glanced out the tall windows of the chapel, at a grove of trees.

"You know," I began, "the trees around this place are beautiful — pine and oak and maple, some tall and some short, all mixed together. And I'm sure you've appreciated their beauty, even those of you who just got here, day before yesterday. They're beautiful, because they're God-made, like so much of what you see around here — beautiful, peaceful, intricately inter-related... Have you ever noticed how everything in the woods seems to fit together? How you can't imagine any one area being any different, because it fits so perfectly with all the rest? That's because God made it and fitted it in with all the rest. They blend perfectly because God loves His creations, and they reflect that love.

"And you're one of His creations, you know.

When He made you, He intended you to fit perfectly with His other creations; you're part of the plan. But He also gave you a free will, and you're the only creature He gave that to. The trees can't decide who they're going to grow next to and who they're not, any more than the animals can change their instincts.

"But you have a choice: you can choose to fit into His forest where He intended you to be, or you can choose not to. He made it voluntary, because He wants you to become His children, not merely His creatures. To become a child of His and have fellowship with Him, you have to freely choose to take the place in the woods that He has chosen for you, and not wander off to another place that might look nicer, or insist on a place He has in mind for someone else, or choose one place this day, another place the next.

"And when you find the place He has for you, you've got another free-will choice: to be a blessing there, to all that is around you, or not. In fact, that's a choice you make many times a day. Did you ever notice how the trees help one another? How they fertilize the ground for each other with their leaves and needles, and protect one another in windstorms?" I smiled as a number of them turned to look out the windows.

"That's one of the reasons why God has brought you here: to show you how to live in harmony with those around you. So that when you leave here, and step into the place He has prepared for you, you'll be a blessing where you're planted."

I pointed to the trees out the window, and now

the rest turned. "They're God-made, and because they are, you can almost feel the love that went into them. Most of you come from environments that are man-made, and some of you have never known anything else. Man doesn't love the things he makes, except in a selfish way, for what they can do for him, or his ego. So most of you don't know what it is to live twenty-four hours a day in an environment where you can almost feel the love around you. That's another reason He has brought you here.

"The great thing is, you can have that same love inside of you, and you can take it with you, wherever you go, even back into the man-made world. Have you ever seen a tree growing in the middle of a city? It's a visual oasis, a reminder of God's love, in a place that doesn't often reflect it.

"That love within is what happens when you open your heart to Jesus, and don't just believe in Him, but be living in Him, and for Him. You can have the same peace and tranquility that you see around you, inside of you, when you give up your own way and choose His, when you are prepared to fit into the woods in the place that He has for you and to live in harmony with those He has placed around you.

"When you have that love within, you'll carry it with you, wherever you go, like some secret, hidden treasure. And if the place He has for you is in the city, you'll be a spiritual oasis there — a place in the desert where people can come for shade and to refresh themselves from living water." It was time to close.

"Many of you have already invited Jesus into

your hearts, but there is still much that He would teach and show you. And to those of you who haven't, He is saying, let me take the burden from you — your life, with all its sin and failures. And I will give you My life, in its place.

"And He'll forgive everything that you have ever done that needs forgiving, if you are truly sorry for it, and ask His forgiveness. And with the blood He already shed for you at Calvary, He'll wash you clean of all your sins, as clean as freshly fallen snow. Why? Because He made you, and He loves you. And He has been waiting all your life for you to realize it.

"He's knocking on the door of your heart, right now, some of you. But there's only one latch on that door, and it's on the inside. All you have to do is open it, but He won't make you, nor will anyone else." It was very quiet in the chapel. "I'm not going to ask anyone to stand up or come forward. Just think about what you've heard. And remember: like those trees, you're God-made, not man-made."

10

A Choice of Realities

That afternoon, after lunch and quiet time, Simon Beteta, Norman Miller and Don McKay, the other interning group leader, called Alpha together for a light session. "We thought it would be a good idea to see how you felt about the weekend, how the ball game went, and how the new guys are settling in. And for the benefit of you three new men, we should explain that since Alpha has been together for quite some time now — Amos and James here, almost three months — the group handles most of its business itself. We group leaders will remain in the background most of the time, and will not intrude, unless we feel it is absolutely necessary." He paused and smiled. "Sometimes it is, to get Larry to speak up. Or Polo not to." And everyone laughed.

"So, all three of you should feel free to speak up. If you've got something you want to say to someone, say it, or if you feel that the Holy Spirit might be giving you an insight into another's problem. Don't worry: if we get the slightest check that what you're saying is not of God, we'll cut you off. This is not an encounter group, nor is it a glorified dump session, and God is not about to let it become one. All it is, is a chance to be real with one another, the way we're supposed to all the time, only seldom are. A light group is not an end in itself; it is merely a beginning — a way for people to begin to be open and honest with one another, which is the way Jesus ultimately wants us to be all the time."

Norman was watching the faces of the new men as Simon spoke, and now he had something to add: "We're called to submit ourselves one to another, and for a lot of us that doesn't come easy; in fact, some of us never did to anyone, not willingly, until we came here. So in a sense, this is spring practice; the opening game comes the day you leave the program."

Now it was Don McKay's turn: "A lot of people would like to believe that they can get all their guidance and truth from God direct, and don't need to have anyone tell them anything. But the truth is, if deep down we really don't *want* to hear something, then 95% of the time we won't hear, no matter how much God might be trying to tell us. And the other 5% of the time, He has to hit us over the head with a mallet. So when your brother tells you something, *listen*; it just might be God."

"Well," said Simon, "how about the weekend?"

This time, there was no self-conscious silence; several people were bubbling over. "I could sure go for s'more smores right now!" Raul grinned, and Keith nodded at the recollection.

"I liked the baseball," Larry said slowly, "Keith taught me — "

"Did you see that fantastic catch I made?" Polo interrupted.

"Did you see how you lofted the ball over the backstop?" Jose retorted, and several others hooted with laughter.

"Hey, said Stas, "let Larry finish."

"Keith taught me how to bat," Larry said falteringly, when they had quieted down. "Nobody ever tried to teach me anything like that before." And he began to get choked up. "But even so, I didn't hit anything."

"Man, that doesn't matter," Jose was speaking now, "You were good up there! I saw you. You took some good cuts at the ball!" Larry smiled through the tears that had begun to form.

After a moment, Raul spoke. "I gotta say it: this place is God's country! It's like the sermon said; you really get the feeling He put it all together, everything with everything else. I even have the feeling He's watching us, and kind of smiling. That He had the deer come back, so we could have a look at them," he shook his head in wonder. "You get an idea of His bigness up here — and yet, how close He is, too." And several of the men nodded.

"What about you, Keith?" Simon asked.

"I like it," Keith said. "I've been to camp for a few years, so I can't get worked up about it the way he can, but I like it."

"Anything in particular?"

113

"Oh, I suppose I like the quiet times the best," he said, recollecting. "But the things we did together were fun, too," he hastened to add.

Stas spoke up now. "Keith, sometimes I think you check out on us, even when we're doing something together. Like when we had to remind you that it was your turn at bat. I mean, *nobody* forgets when they're the next man to the plate!"

Keith looked at Stas, starting to frown. He was about to say something, when Raul spoke. "It's true, Keith. A lot of times, you're only half there when I talk to you. Like the other morning, on the way back from the bathroom. You mumbled something about different realities — I still don't know what you meant."

Embarrassed to suddenly be the center of attention, Keith was at a loss for words.

"Where do you go, when you check out?" Simon asked gently, to help him out.

"I don't know," said Keith, making an effort to answer the question. "I guess I just — drift." He frowned. "Do you suppose we could change the subject?"

"You mean, get off your back?" Stas asked. "Didn't you hear them, man? We're not out to get you; we're actually trying to help you. Because there's obviously something here that you can't see."

"Or don't want to see," suggested Amos, who rarely spoke. "Like *why* you started drifting in the first place."

"You know, it might have something to do with why you drink the way you do," said Simon. "In fact, it wouldn't surprise me if the drifting started before the drinking. Is that right?"

Keith thought a moment, then nodded, as interested now as they were.

"What is he most interested in, when he talks about things?" Simon asked the group.

"That's easy," piped up Polo, "motorbikes. One time, when we were at the Brooklyn center, our group went somewhere in a van. I can't remember what we were doing then. But I do remember that every bike we passed, he could tell you what year and make it was, and what were its good points and weak points."

"Yeah," Raul concurred, "about the only thing I've heard him mention of his old life was his bike. Like he really missed it. Oh, and his sister Kathy being nuts about horses. He mentioned that once."

"*Why* do you like your bike so much?" Simon asked.

Keith shrugged. "I don't know; I just like to get on it and ride."

"Come on, man, you can do better than that," encouraged Norman. "Could be, riding is a form of drifting?"

Keith brightened. "You know, I'd never thought of that, exactly, but it's true. When you're riding, and you're not in a hurry, you're just sort of floating — taking in the scenery, let whatever happens, happen. Hills come and go, curves, flatlands, bridges ..." His voice took on a dream-like quality, a half-smile playing on his lips. Stas started to speak, but Simon signalled him to wait.

"You're just purring along," Keith continued, "kind of cozy-like; the only sound you notice is when your tires go to a different surface, like

115

from a metal bridge back to asphalt. Cars and trucks come and go, and it's like you're there, but you're also watching it all from somewhere else, you know what I mean?'' Almost all of them nodded; though possibly none of them had ever owned a bike, they had been on enough trips of other kinds, to know whereof he spoke.

"Sometimes, another biker comes along, and if he's going your way, and you like the way he's riding, maybe you'll ride along together. Sometimes, you stop for gas and a couple of beers, but basically that's an interruption, not a destination. People don't understand that: they think we ride because we want to get somewhere. But that's not it at all; the destination is merely the excuse for the going. Once you get there, it's almost invariably a disappointment.'' He coasted to a stop. "You know, I've never talked about it this way before," he said, wonderingly.

"He's not an alcoholic!" said Ray abrasively, "he's a bike freak! A bike-aholic!" and he laughed, but no one joined in.

"That's out of order!" Norman spoke out sharply.

"Keith, why do you think you're so anxious to ride?" Simon asked quietly. "And then when you stop somewhere, you're so anxious to get going again?"

"Okay," Keith smiled, "why?"

"Maybe it's because you can't bear the reality you're stuck in. As long as you're on your bike, there's as least the faint hope that somewhere down the road, there's something better than what lies behind you. There never is, of course;

116

each time you touch down, it's just as grubby as the last time, though it may take a different form. But as long as you're moving, you don't have to look at that. And after a while, after enough disappointments, enough hurts, you get so you avoid thinking down the road ahead; you just concentrate on the road itself — *that* part's all right." He stopped, and there was a long silence. God, the Master Economist, was speaking to many hearts.

"Does that witness to you?" Simon asked at length, and Keith nodded, without speaking.

Simon looked around the group. "You know it's not just bikes. It's whatever you use to take leave of reality — dope or glue or pot or sex or alcohol. You take your trip for the same reason Keith gets on his bike: your reality is as unbearable as his is. And you know, a lot of straight people have a lot of socially acceptable ways of escaping their realities, too. Know anyone who watches TV all the time? Or is all the time eating or nibbling? Or on the phone? Or even sleeping?" A number of heads bobbed in assent.

"You can even escape into a virtue, like work," Simon went on. "I know of several workaholics who spend far more time at the office than they really have to, totally immersed in commendable and justifiable hard labor, because underneath they can't bear to face the reality that awaits them at home."

Simon was silent for a moment, to give them a chance to assimilate. "What is it about reality that makes it so unbearable?" he finally asked.

"Why will people do anything to keep from contemplating it? Because reality, without Christ, is one gigantic zero. Without Him, life is ultimately so pointless that it doesn't bear looking at. To contemplate it, face on, is to go mad or kill oneself. And so, our countless, endless escape mechanisms are merely our subconscious, trying to protect us from a truth that would blow out all our fuses."

Stas broke the long silence. That's pretty heavy."

Simon nodded. "Let's get back to Keith," he said. And then, looking at him, "A while back, you said, 'people don't understand' — by people, did you mean your parents?"

"I guess so. I really didn't think much about it."

"Well, it could be that your relationship with them is where your reality began to become unbearable. Do they love you?"

"Very much," said Keith quickly.

"Do they understand you?"

He didn't answer right away. "They try to," he said at length.

"Is your father happy about your drifting?" Keith shook his head. "What do you think he wants you to do?"

"Make something of myself."

"Anything specific?"

"I think there were some specifics in the beginning, but at this point, I think he'd settle for anything — as long as it was 'a worthy ambition.' "

"So you and your father don't get along," Simon stated.

118

"I wouldn't put it that way. We get along fine, as long as I don't mention motorbikes or liquor and seem to be busy."

"But you ride a lot, and daydream a lot, and drink whenever you can." Keith nodded, and Simon looked at him, before continuing. "Because you can never be like him, no matter how hard you try, and somewhere along the line you realized that and gave up trying." Keith gave no indication that he had heard, but just stared at the floor in front of him. "And yet, that doesn't stop you from wanting his approval as badly as ever." Still no response. "And so your reality becomes unbearable." Keith passed a hand over his eyes, and avoided looking up.

"You know," said Simon, going over and putting an arm around him, "there is a way out of this. Bring someone into your life whose approval is more important to you than your father's. Let Jesus in, Keith. This other is just tearing you apart." Keith nodded and gave an involuntary sob and buried his head in Simon's side. Simon just held Keith, as he wept, and the rest of the group remained silent. But there were tears in more than a few eyes.

"Do you want to turn your life over to God?" Simon asked after a while.

"Yes," Keith said, looking up and smiling, as he wiped his eyes.

"Then say this prayer after me: Lord Jesus," and he waited for Keith to repeat the words. "I've done a lot of things I'm ashamed of. And I'm sorry. Forgive me, Lord. And cleanse me with your blood. I accept your forgiveness and your bloodwashing. And I ask you, Lord Jesus, to come into my heart with the fullness of your Spirit, and dwell within me forever. I give you my life. From now on, it's yours, not mine. Hallelujah!"

When Keith said the last, he looked up and laughed. "That's the first time I've ever said 'hallelujah.' *Hallelujah!*"

"Well, it certainly won't be the last!" Norman exclaimed, coming over to give him a hug. "You feel any different?"

"Not really. Except that I feel all hollowed out inside, like I've been scoured out from head to foot with a Brillo pad. But it's good." And then he started to laugh. "I'm so happy, I'm afraid I'm going to start crying again," and he turned his face away.

"Never be ashamed of tears," Simon said. "Someone far wiser than me once called them 'the window washing of the soul'." He smiled. "Feel sorry for the man who *can't* cry."

"Whew!" gasped Keith, when the tears finally began to subside. "I never thought it was possible to feel this way!" He looked up at all of them. "Thanks," he said, and started to cry again. Don had slipped out of the room, and now came back with a box of Kleenex, which he handed to Keith. " Don't be concerned about our friend here. Just let him bawl." They all laughed, and Keith along with them. "Those tears are part of the healing that God had begun deep inside of him, and it's going to take a while."

"Um, would you pray for me, too?" Polo suddenly asked, in a voice much meeker than anything they had ever heard from him.

"Yeah, and me," said Larry.

"I've accepted Jesus," said Raul, "but I'd still like you to pray for me."

Simon glanced over at Ray, who had remained silent through the whole proceeding. "No, man, not now," Ray said, trying to keep it casual. But he was too badly shaken to carry it off.

"Come on, Ray," young James said. "Forget about being cool, and get it on!"

"You guys are crazy!" burst out Ray, startling them all. "You let these three sweet-talk you into giving up your lives, and now you're just like putty in their hands. Well, I got news for you: no sweet-talking Christian jive-artists are ever going to make a fool out of Razor Daniels!" And with that, he stormed out of the room.

"Ray!" Stas started after him. "Come back!"

"No," said Simon, catching him by the arm, "let him go. The state he's in, he couldn't possibly hear you. The Old Boy's got his reins now, and he's hell-bent for the Rock. But trust the Lord. God's still in charge, and He knows what He's doing. For the first time since he joined the program, Ray has just been totally honest with the rest of us. I have a feeling we haven't seen the last of Mr. Daniels."

Ray did not leave that evening, physically. He had no money, and it would have been almost impossible for him to hitchhike back into the city. But there was no doubt that he had left mentally, and the next weekend, when Alpha went in to help the Brooklyn center get a special mailing out, he made his move.

The groups had gone in early, because that

Friday afternoon, Raul's case had finally come up, and he was due in court at three o'clock. Usually, when a man in the program went before a judge, Joe or his senior group leader would go with him, or possibly Randy. In this situation, which seemed so hopeless, the others felt, and I agreed, that I was supposed to go.

John Pagon met us shortly before we were due to go in, and the three of us prayed and released the whole thing to God. And that afternoon, in that courtroom, the Lord gave us favor. Raul told the judge the truth, and the truth about what had happened in his heart as well, and the Judge believed him. He was remanded into our custody, on condition that he complete the program.

That evening, helping the others to fold and stuff the mailing, Raul was jubilant, his spirit soaring through the heavenlies. And the more joyful he seemed to get, the darker became Ray, who was sitting next to him. Sometime after lights out, he split.

11

He Who Lives by the Sword . . .

Closing the door to 416 quietly behind him, Ray headed for the Clinton and Washington subway station. He was carrying what clothes he had with him in a second-hand cardboard suitcase, and he was walking fast. At that hour in the early morning, the subway platform was deserted; looking the attendant in the eye, as if challenging him to do something about it, Ray easily vaulted the turnstile. "Hey!" shouted the attendant, as Ray walked down the platform, "What do you think you're doing?" But he made no move to leave the safety of his booth.

Down on the platform, Ray paced back and forth, muttering to himself and smashing his right fist into his left palm. When the A train came at last, he stepped on and stood up, reading the car cards, though he could have had any seat in the car. Almost any seat, save two in the corner, where three leather-jacketed white youths were giggling. One of them was completely wasted, eyes glazed, mouth hanging open, and the other two were high on something.

123

They looked up at him, and then sniggered and looked at him again, saying something, the meaning of which was perfectly clear even if Ray couldn't hear the words. Ray's jaw clenched, and he went over to them. "You got something to say to me?" he asked quietly.

"Well, you know, we just might," said the largest of the three. "What do you think, Huey, have we got something to say to him?" and his hand started for his jacket pocket.

Using the edge of his palm in a backhanded sweep, Ray caught him in the neck and sent him backwards over the seat. As his companion jumped on Ray, he brought his other elbow up, catching his assailant under the chin, and almost lifting him off his feet. The youth cried out and clapped a hand to his mouth, bringing it away with pieces of teeth in it, and a jagged, bloody mess where his teeth used to be. The third youth just looked up at Ray and vacantly shook his head, waving his hands back and forth in front of his face.

Ray looked down at the leader who was rubbing his neck and getting to his feet. "Like I said," Ray continued, breathing only slightly heavily, "do you punks want to rap?"

The leader shook his head. "No, man, we got nothing to say."

"Then get out of this car." And the two who could walk, lifted their companion and made their way into the next car, the one called Huey holding his free hand over his mouth.

Ray smiled to himself and went back to reading the car cards, until the train reached the station he

124

wanted, about six blocks from Sal's apartment on Avenue A. When he reached the street level, it was deserted, and he started walking quickly. Just then, he heard something behind him and glanced over his shoulder, to see two dark forms coming at him, the blade of a knife glinting in the pale light of an overhead streetlamp. He tried to pivot to avoid it, but it was too late; it plunged into his side, just beneath the rib cage.

"Agh!" Ray grunted, as his attacker jerked the blade out and made ready to use it again. Clutching his side, Ray swung the suitcase blindly in front of him, hitting the hand that held the knife and sending it skittering away into the shadows. "Come on, Huey, I stuck him good; let's get outa here!"

"Well, lemme get a phot at the baphard; I owe him one!" responded the other through broken teeth, and he punched Ray in the side, where he had just been stabbed. Ray screamed and doubled over in pain but did not go down, and as the one called Huey closed in for another shot, Ray aimed a straight kick at his kneecap, which caused him to cry out in pain.

"Come on!" shouted the leader, "I told you to get outa here!" And without waiting, he took off, Huey limping along behind.

Ray sagged against the lamppost and started to throw up. He held his hand up under the light: it was covered with blood. Fumbling open the suitcase and taking out a shirt, he pressed it against his side. Then, holding it there, he tried to walk. The suitcase was now more than he could manage, and he threw it in a trash receptacle.

The six blocks to Sal's took an eternity. Towards the end, he was stopping to rest at every lamppost, and spending more time resting than walking. But the worst was yet to come: Sal's apartment was a three-floor walk up. In the foyer, he rang her bell, but there was no answer. Ray looked at his watch, blinked, and tried to focus: twenty minutes to two. She wouldn't be home from the club where she worked for another hour yet.

Cursing under his breath, he was about to turn away, to see if he could somehow reach the fire escape outside, when two young kids suddenly opened the door. Clearly bent on some night work of their own, they paid no attention to him, and he was able to slip inside, before the door closed. Up the stairs he went, dizzy now, and having to wait every few steps for his head to clear. The door to her apartment was locked, of course, and rather than break it in and arouse everyone in the building — provided he *could* break it in, which in his present condition was doubtful — he headed for the roof. The door was open, and he woozily made his way to the fire escape and down it, several times losing his balance and staggering into the railing.

Somehow he made it back down to her window, but he lost the shirt which he had been holding against his side, and now the blood was flowing with every move he made. He was starting to gray out, and knew he had only a couple of minutes left at best, to get inside. With his elbow, he smashed the window just below the catch and reached in to unlock it. With all his remaining strength, he pushed the window up, and fell into the room, lying still on the floor.

Time passed, and he revived, crawling over to the bed and reaching under it. The black leather suitcase was still there, where he'd left it. He got it open, groped around inside, and pulled out the long-barreled .44. Then, he heaved himself up on the bed. It was unmade, and he wadded the top sheet and pressed it against his side. "Place is a mess," he muttered and passed out.

At the sound of a key in the door, Ray revived. There were muffled voices in the hall, Sal's and somebody else's. The door opened, Sal stepped in and turned on the light — and shrieked. "Razor! What are you doing here? Oh my God, look at the blood!" For there was blood everywhere, on the floor, over by the window, on the bed, and all over Ray. "Get rid of him, baby," he managed, nodding toward the well-dressed white man who stood behind her, out in the hall.

The white man spoke up. "Maybe *you're* the one who should leave," he said, stepping inside. "This is Sally's place, and you've obviously upset — " his voice trailed off, as he came into view of Ray, the bloodstains, and the .44 that was slowly being leveled at his chest. His eyes widened and his mouth began to work, but no sound would come out. Sal turned him around and headed him out the door. "I think you'd better go, Ted," and he nodded, his steps soon audible, clattering down the stairs.

"Sugar! What happened! We gotta get you to

a hospital!" But Ray shook his head. "How hot am I?" he asked.

"The papers aren't talking about the Black Hat Bandit any more, but the man is looking for him all over the city. You were right, though: not one of them mentioned the scar on your face." Ray chuckled weakly and then winced, holding his side.

"Yeah, but do they know it's old Razor?" he wheezed.

"No. The only one looking for you is your P.O., with a warrant for your violating parole. He's been by here several times, hoping to catch you, but apparently it's not important enough for them to put this place under surveillance, or they would have been up here by now."

"Then the hospital's out. They've got to report knife wounds, and they would connect it up just like that," he tried to snap his fingers, but the effort was too much for him.

"Well, what are we going to do, Daddy? We can't just let you bleed to death!" and she bit her lip to keep from crying.

"We're not going to. First, get a pan, soapy water, and a clean sponge — that is, if you can find one around this place. Then clean up the wound. Do you still have some gin?" She nodded, and started to get him a glass. "Not to drink, stupid," he gasped, "to pour into the hole. Now listen, because I'm about to pass out again. Tear up a bedsheet in strips — a clean one — and wrap it around me many times, tight as you can. First thing in the morning, go out and get some tape and bandages and strong antiseptic.

128

Now go get me some water." But before she could do so, he had passed out.

His hand fell away from his side, and she could see the hole, and the dark blood welling out of it. She stared at it, and pressed the back of her hand against her mouth, then hurried to do as he had instructed.

The next thing Ray knew, it was daylight. Sal had drawn the shade, but the window was broken, and it was flapping in the breeze, the sun behind it flashing intermittently into the room. "Ahh," Ray groaned, as he tried to move. He was barely able to lift his head, but he smiled at what he saw; she had swathed him in bedsheet from his armpits to his hips. And tight, too; he could scarcely breathe. "Mama, this is cool," he whispered. But even so, there was a red stain half way down his left side.

"Sal?" he called out. No answer. "Must be getting that stuff," he muttered, and went back to sleep. The next time he opened his eyes, she was there, sitting by the bed, watching him. She still had her evening dress on. "Oh, honey, it's good to see you awake!" she said, grabbing his hand and kissing it.

"You got the bandages?" She nodded. "Then let's get it on," he said, rolling over, to make it easier for her. "Never mind unwrapping the sheet," he said. "Get a sharp kitchen knife and just cut through it." And she did.

When the wound was laid bare, Ray told her to put plenty of antiseptic on it, and she poured it on, though he hollered like a bull. Then she put the fresh bandage on it and taped it up. When she was finished, her hands were shaking, but Ray took them, and smiled. "You know what? I think I'm going to live. But Mama, I'm awful thirsty. Bring me water and some orange juice, if you've got any."

"Orange juice? I haven't had any of that stuff since I stopped living with my mother, five years ago."

"Well, get some, because I don't want to take anything solid for awhile, until I'm healed inside."

So she went out, and Ray drank as much water as he could and then slept. The next time he woke up, there was a large pitcher of orange juice beside the bed. Sal was there, too, and she was worried.

"Honey, everybody in the street is talking about the bloodstains over by the subway, and the suitcase in the trash can with blood on it, and the blood on the sidewalk leading this way. They don't know exactly where it stops, but the police are asking everyone in all the tenements, if they heard or saw anything."

Ray thought a moment, reviewing the contents of the suitcase. "There wasn't anything in that suitcase they could tie to me, except — oh, no! I'd taken that course book from Teen Challenge with me, as a souvenir!" He shook his head. "It had my name in it. How could I be so stupid!"

"You weren't stupid, honey. How'd you know you were going to get knifed?"

"Well, it will still be a while before they can

trace me," he said, calming down. "Let's have some of the O.J." And she poured him a tall glass.

"You know," he said, sipping it, "I had the craziest dream, this last time. Up at that camp I was at, there was a big lake, and we went down to it at night, to see some deer. There was a full moon, so it was pretty bright, but it was still spooky. Well, I dreamed that I was back at the lake, and down by the water's edge, and I looked along the shore, and there was this thing, maybe a hundred yards away, looking at me. It wasn't a deer, like before; it had dark red eyes that seemed to glow — "

Sal shuddered. "Do you have to go on, honey? It's giving me the creeps."

"It scared me, too, baby," Ray admitted. "Worse than anything since I was a little boy down in Carolina."

He took another swallow. "But there was also a mist on the lake — all silvery, and somehow *it* wasn't scarey. In fact, it seemed to drift in and come all around me, hiding me and protecting me from that thing with the red eyes. And while the mist was all around me, I felt someone touch my side and hold their hand there, for a moment. And then I woke up." He put the orange juice down. "I wonder what it means? I have the funniest feeling it's all tied together — the camp, the course book, the guys from the subway. . ." His voice drifted off.

"Don't think about it, honey; it gives me the willies, when you talk that way. Hey," she said, running her finger over his chin, "speaking of

131

eyes, did you see how big that white boy's eyes got, when he saw you and the gun on the bed? He was so scared, I thought he was going to — "

"Don't," Ray said, chuckling and then wincing, as Sal laughed.

Two days later, Ray walked in the front door of 444 Clinton.

"Is Mr. Revish in?" he asked the receptionist. "I got to see him."

"Who shall I say is calling?" she asked, reaching for the intercom.

"Raze — uh, Ray Daniels. And tell him it's urgent."

12

Welcome Back, Daniels

The door to Joe Revish's office opened, and in came Ray Daniels, a big smile on his face, just as if he had never left. But there did not seem to be quite as much wind in his sails this time, and he waited to be invited, before sitting down.

"Well," Joe said.

"I've come back."

"I see that. Do you remember me telling you that re-entering the program wasn't that easy? That you would first have to convince us that you have had a real heart change, and then you would have to wait until there was an opening? That even when there was an opening, you would have to start all over again from scratch?" Ray nodded.

"But you think you have some circumstances so extraordinary, I'll bend regulations, is that it?" Ray nodded again.

"Well, let's hear them," Joe said, trying to keep from smiling.

Ray cleared his throat. "Mr. Revish, when I left here, I was mad! Burning mad!"

"So I heard."

"And I stayed mad, all the way to the subway. But when I got on the subway and started to ride toward my girlfriend's, I began to calm down. And as I listened to the train wheels, when they were screeching on the rails underneath the city, I began to hear a voice. 'Go back, Ray,' the voice was saying — it called me Ray, not Razor," he said with great sincerity, and Joe had to dig his thumbnail into the palm of his other hand, to keep a straight face. "Go on," he said.

"Well, sir, after I got off of that subway, I could hear that voice more clearly, because there was no one else around, nothing but the sound of my shoes on the sidewalk. 'Go back, go back, go back,' the voice seemed to be saying, in time with my footsteps."

"Mmm," Joe nodded, as if weighing the footstep-voice against other voices that had been reported to him.

"But my pride was too great to come back right then," Ray continued. "For three days, I fought the memory of that voice, but I couldn't get it out of my mind, no matter how hard I tried. And so," he concluded, extending his hands, palms upward, "here I am."

"So?"

Ray frowned; he had expected more of a response than that. "Well," he said, "I feel God wants me here, and so who am I to fight God?"

"Or me either," Joe murmured, too low for Ray to hear. "Ray, I'm going to level with you,"

134

he said, looking him in the eye. "Everything in me tells me that you're still conning, all the way. I'm being had, and I know it, but . . ."

"But there's the remotest possibility that I might be telling the truth," he said, completing Joe's sentence with a grin. "And you can't afford to take that chance, right?"

"Right. And you *knew* I couldn't, didn't you!"

"Mr. Revish," he said, suddenly the soul of innocence, "you're not going to regret it, sir! *God* is in this, Mr. Revish, and you're going to be happily surprised."

Joe smiled, as he stood up. "You know, I believe He is, Ray, and you may find yourself even more surprised than I am. You can wait outside."

When he had left, Joe called Randy on the intercom. "Guess who was just in my office?"

"I know; I saw him go in," Randy replied.

"Well," said Joe with a chuckle, "I think I've just been royally conned, but I'd like to reinstate him in the program."

"I'm glad, Joe."

"Me, too," Joe replied.

There *was* a difference in Ray, in those days before he was due to be transferred back into Alpha group — minute, almost imperceptible, but it was there. He still had all the right answers, but there seemed to be a softening around the edges. And perhaps it was a result of the light sessions, and his growing awareness that the staff

135

could see right through him anyway, but it no longer seemed so important to him to maintain his Mr. Cool image. He could relax and begin to enjoy what he was doing, or not enjoy it, as the case might be. In short, he could begin to be real.

Something else may have affected him, as well; he could not have failed to notice the change in both Raul and Keith, during those last days they had been together. Aside from their growing joy and peace, which at the time had so irritated him, they had become more sensitive to where others were at, and Ray, who was exceptionally sensitive himself, had to be computing all of that.

The change in his own attitude was so slight that it might have gone unnoticed, were the staff not looking for it. In the classroom, he was not quite so quick to belittle; indeed, he seemed to do less talking and more listening than before. On the work program, he did an honest job, actually trying to do what was asked of him to the best of his ability. But probably the most significant of these nuances surfaced in Genesis group's light sessions. Before, Ray had refused to enter in, remaining aloof, judgmental, disdainful, and if he spoke, it was usually to put somebody down, even if he believed that he was only trying to be helpful, and got angry when the group leaders called him on it. For Ray had a natural gift of discernment which had been developed in all his years of fronting it; he knew why people responded as they did, and he knew how to use that knowledge to hurt them.

But now, Ray was not mocking. He still was not participating or taking an active role in the light sessions, but he was listening. And sometimes, he would step in to keep certain sharp-tongued individuals from doing unto others what he had formerly been guilty of himself. Like the time the group was talking to Carlos. (In preparation for what they would soon be experiencing at Camp Champion, Hector and Charles and Don, the three group leaders, were encouraging the group to resolve its own problems, with the three of them ready to step in whenever needed — God's referees, as it were.)

"Oh, come on, man!" Carlos was saying. "Why are you guys making such a big deal out of it? I was only kidding."

"No you weren't," said Charles, trying to explain it to him. "You were putting Tony down and then tagging a laugh on it, so that people would laugh with you. And if Tony himself didn't at least crack a smile, then he couldn't take a 'joke'. It's a very dirty way of fighting."

"Man, you are *crazy!*" shouted Carlos. "You are blowing smoke, for sure! I — "

"Listen to the man," Ray cut in. "He's not jivin' you."

Startled, Carlos shut up. Then he looked over at Hector.

"Humor can be sharper than a scalpel, when it's used the wrong way," Hector allowed. "Carlos, your tongue has been your equalizer all your life. You've made up for your smallness in stature by largeness of mouth, and you can cut somebody with you humor, so quick that they won't even know they've been stabbed, until they happen to look down and see blood spurting out in six different directions."

"But now that you've turned your life over to

137

the Lord," Charles added, "He wants you to clean up your act. So it's good that the guys care enough about you, to let you know you're slicing someone, so you can see what your humor does to others."

It was Hector who spoke again: "And don't *you* go getting your feelings hurt, when they speak to you. Because, believe it or not, that's what love between Christian brothers is really all about. If instead, they ignored your sin, because they didn't want to bother coming against your flak, and then excused it on the ground of being 'loving Christians', how would you know what it did to other people? Would it really be more loving to leave you stuck in a sin that you were blind to?"

"But this is the way I *talk*!" Carlos burst out. "How am I going to change that?"

"You can't," said Charles matter-of-factly. "But the Holy Spirit can. Give Him permission, and then trust Him to operate through the other guys, and cooperate with Him."

Carlos thought about that, and it was obvious that he was struggling with it. "Okay, you guys!" he finally burst out, "you can give me the business when I stick it to someone else with a laugh. But I'm warning you: the first guy who takes advantage, it's off with the gloves. I'll clean your clock before you know what time it is!" And everyone laughed.

The day before Ray was due to transfer back to Alpha group at Camp Champion, Randy's intercom buzzed. It was Joe: "I've got a situation

138

here that's pretty serious. Seems our friend Ray is in violation of parole, and is wanted for questioning in connection with an apparent assault, and possibly murder. His parole officer is waiting outside my office now and has a warrant for him, and I gather he has some notions of yanking him right now. Anyway, I think you ought to see him."

"Yup, I'll be down right away."

The man was not known to Randy. He had a battered suitcase with him, and was very businesslike, insisting on showing his identification, though Randy had initially waved it aside. "We have reason to believe that you have a Ray Daniels, also known as Razor Daniels, now enrolled in your program."

"That is correct," said Randy, equally formal. "Is he in any trouble?"

"That's putting it mildly," and he told Randy and Joe of the parole violation and what concerned them even more: the suitcase covered with blood, and the trail of blood that led to the apartment of his girlfriend. "The girl, of course, denied that Daniels had been there for weeks. But I watched her when I mentioned Teen Challenge, and her tilt meter definitely lit up. He had been there, all right; in fact, I must have just missed him, a couple of times. But what I want to know is: what about all that blood? We finally found someone who admitted that they heard a scuffle on the street late Friday night, but no gunshots. So the wound had to be inflicted by a knife — or razor. What was it all about? Was Daniels the inflic*tor* or the inflic*tee*?"

139

Randy shrugged. "I'm as much in the dark as you are. But look: we want to cooperate with you in any way that we can. Just tell us what you would have us do."

The parole officer seemed a little surprised at that. "Well," he said, taking a more amenable tone, "I was going to take him with me, right now. But if you're willing to, you could have someone bring him over to the court house this afternoon, around three. I want to talk to him about that blood. And as for the parole, from what I've heard from Judge Walker, and a couple of other people who know Teen Challenge, we might be able to arrange something, *if* he stays in your program for a year."

"Well, at the moment," Randy replied, as honestly as he could, "that's questionable. Because he dropped out, and we bent a rule to take him back. And now it turns out that he lied through his teeth, in order to get back in. But I'll talk to him. And one way or another, we'll have him there at three o'clock."

After the parole officer had left, Joe and Randy sent for Ray. He came in smiling, but was also scrutinizing their faces, though trying to appear not to be doing so.

Randy was in no mood for playing games. "They found the suitcase, Ray," he said bluntly. "Now what *really* happened?"

As Ray sat down, he winced, all trace of a smile gone. "So you were the inflictee," Randy mused.

"All right, spill it," Joe said, "and this time, leave out the mysterious voices."

"There's not much to tell," Ray said flatly, his

140

eyes on the floor in front of him. "On the subway, I cleaned up on a couple of white dudes who thought they were big enough to take me. Then they jumped me from behind after I got off the subway, and one of them stuck me with a shank. I made it to my girlfriend's and laid up there, a couple of days. Then I came back."

"Has a doctor seen your wound?" Ray shook his head. "Then as soon as we're done, someone's going to take you over to Cumberland Hospital and have your side looked at. I don't want you getting infected and dying around here. It would bring the place a bad name." Randy didn't smile, and neither did Ray.

"Ray," he asked abruptly, "how do you really feel about the program? And I want a straight answer. If I so much as suspect that you're gaming — "

Ray nodded. "I don't like being told what to do. But then, I never did, anywhere. And this sure beats jail. I used to think that all that Jesus stuff was the biggest con there was: 'There'll be pie in the sky when you die, and in the meantime, be a good boy and do what Miss Anne or Massah Bob tells you.' My mother had bought that con, and I wasn't about to." His anger subsided as quickly as it had flared up.

"But now, I don't know. I'm not blind; I could see what happened to the other guys. It's good. And maybe it'll be good for me, too. That's as far as I can go; more than that, and I'd be putting you on."

Randy stood up. "Okay, I believe you. Milton will take you over to the courthouse this

141

afternoon. I want you to tell your P.O. and the judge exactly what you've told me. No more, no less.''

When Randy called me to tell me what had happened, it was the sort of news I could appreciate, at that moment. I had just gotten through taking a phone call from Keith Lawson's father, who had insisted that he would not talk to anyone else. No sooner had he said hello, than he started in: "My wife and I want to see our son," he said.

"Well, Mr. Lawson, he's just been transferred up to Camp Champion, and it's our policy to discourage visits from relatives and friends during the first six weeks that a student is in the program. In many cases, it's a difficult period of adjustment. They've just begun learning a new way of living, and it could be a serious jolt to them, to expose them to such a strong pull from their old way of life. Now it happens that Keith is making a very good adjustment, but we can't — "

"Are you telling me I can't see my son?" he interrupted, as angry as if I had said nothing.

"No, but I am strongly advising against it, at this time. We'll be having visitors' days on Sundays, the end of this month and the beginning of August; why don't you and Keith's mother drive up and see him then?"

There was some whispering in the background, which sounded like a woman's voice, and I sensed that it was Mrs. Lawson, and that she had instigated the call. If so, she had either gone to his office, or he had come home early. I prayed for wisdom.

"Look," said Mr. Lawson, his voice strained. "I want you to know that if you're trying to brainwash my son, turn him into some kind of Jesus freak, I'll take him out of there so fast —"

"And do what, Mr. Lawson?" I said, getting angry, in spite of myself, "see him go to jail? Is that how far you'd — " I bit my lip. "I'm sorry," I said, meaning it. "We're trying to do our best for Keith, and he's responding. Please give us a free hand; and when you see him, I know you'll be pleased with the results."

"I'm sorry, too," he said, and there was more whispering in the background. "We'll come up the first Sunday in August."

"Good, I'll look forward to seeing you. And so will Keith." I said goodbye and hung up, only to have Randy call with the news about Ray. He called again a few hours later, to say that they had agreed to let Ray stay in the program.

13

The Jesus Connection

Three days before that first Sunday in August, it did not look like Keith was going to have any visitors at all. Raul came to the group leaders' counseling office, and said that he wanted to talk to him about Keith. It was all he could do to bring himself to speak, and Simon was dismayed to see that he seemed to have reverted back to where he had been when he first came into the program. It turned out that Raul had happened on Keith while he was smoking, and when he confronted him, Keith had told him to buzz off, in much cruder words. But now, Raul, having turned in his friend, was on the verge of tears.

"Raul, listen," Simon said calmly. "You have not betrayed Keith. You have just shown him more love than probably anyone else in this camp. Haven't you seen how increasingly uptight he was getting, the closer his parents' visit came? And man, there was nothing any of us could do to help him. Except pray that the Lord would give us something through which we could reach him.

And now, thanks to your obedience, I think He has."

That afternoon, Simon called Alpha together for a group meeting. He wasted no time getting to the point: "Keith, you've been smoking. Let's have the details." Keith shot a look at Raul, and Simon said, "You lay a guilt trip on him, and I'll lay something on you, about the size of a two-by-four! Now start talking, fast!"

Keith looked at him sullenly, obviously contemplating his three alternatives: total rebellion and leaving, attempting to stonewall it in silence, or minimal compliance. To the intense but unexpressed relief of the group leaders, he chose the last. He was defiant at times, even insulting, but at least he was finally talking.

"You *want* me to leave, don't you?" he was saying.

"If you leave, that will be your decision, not ours," Simon replied calmly. "But once you go out that front gate, you're on your own, pal. Now what about those cigarettes? Where'd you get them?"

"In Point Jervis, when we stopped for gas on the way back from the last Brooklyn trip."

"How many packs?"

"A carton."

"A carton! How many do you have left?"

"Three packs." The defiance had drained out of his voice now; all that was left was a resigned hopelessness.

Simon calculated for a moment. "Just enough to get you through your parents' visit, right?" He nodded. "Where'd you hide them?"

146

"In a dry place, under the porch of the house."

"Was Raul the only one who knew about your smoking?"

"Yes. He came looking for me one afternoon, and he found me, all right." He looked down at the floor. "I knew he'd tell, sooner or later."

"You ought to be glad he did!" Simon said, momentarily angry again. "Come to think of it, you probably are, aren't you?" He thought a moment, then nodded.

Simon took a softer tack, then: "Do you know why you started smoking?"

He shook his head.

"You think it might have had something to do with your parents' coming?" He nodded. "Well, then, why don't you tell us about your feelings?"

"What's to tell?" He sighed. "They're not going to understand, that's all."

"Not going to understand what?" Simon persevered gently.

"I don't know — this place . . . the way I feel now . . . God . . . ." His voice trailed off, and he just shook his head.

"You know, Keith, you're not trusting God at all. This is His place, and you're His son now. Don't you think He's capable of changing your parents' hearts? He changed yours, didn't He?" He nodded. "Well, take a look at your anxiety; it's really unbelief, not believing that God is in charge of the situation. And you know, the sad thing is, how long you've been miserable over this thing — too proud to be needy and ask for help. You're a jerk, you know that?" and he smiled and said, "Yeah."

147

"Remember this, when they come," Simon said finally. "Until they make the connection themselves, there's no way they're going to understand what — or Who — motivates this place, or why we do the things we do. So don't even try to reach them through their heads. The more you try to explain, the more they'll debate with you, point by point. And don't try to evangelize them, either. Because right now Jesus is a major threat to them. For if what you now believe and are trying to live is right, then everything that they have invested so much of their lives in, without Christ, is so much wood, hay and stubble. And that's hard for anyone to admit."

Keith began to see it, and so did several of the others, for their own parents. "So forget about convincing them," Simon concluded. "Just love them. Because ultimately, they will be reached through their hearts. And it could start by their hearts responding to what's happened in your own heart, regardless of what their heads might tell them."

Keith chuckled: "I can just imagine what my father would say to *that*! But I know you're right. Thanks. Thanks very much." He glanced over at Raul. "You, too." And tears sprang again to Raul's eyes.

"But we still have the matter of the cigarettes," Simon said. "Though you see now that they were a pretty sorry substitute for turning to Christ with your problem, you still broke your agreement, and the group needs to decide what should be done about that."

One of the group suggested that Keith be

148

campused, which would mean no trips into town, no phone calls, and no visitors. But Stas spoke up: "I don't think so. The man has really repented, and I doubt very much that he'll ever smoke again. I think we should forget about it. But if it ever happens again —" and the rest laughed.

"Okay," Simon said, and he turned to Keith. "Your parents will be getting here around one on Sunday. Now give the whole thing over to the Lord, trust the Holy Spirit to give you the right words, and just love them."

"You make it sound easy," said Keith, trying to smile.

"You won't know how easy, until you try it," Simon replied.

At precisely one o'clock, the big gray Continental swung into the camp's driveway. "Just like my father," Keith smiled, glancing at his watch, "punctual to the minute." He got up from the steps of the admin building where he had been waiting, and walked down the path to the parking lot, past the old tree stump, where they let him put some corn for the deer. His father was the first out of the car. "Hello!" he said, in his big cheerful way, and he gave Keith a firm handshake. "Hello!" Keith said back, in the identical way. It was a ritual they had perfected over the years that helped bridge the first awkward moments of re-uniting. "Hi!" his mother said warmly and gave him a hug, as he said, "Hi, Mom" back.

"You've gotten a haircut!" she said, holding

149

him at arm's length to admire it. "I wouldn't recognize you at a distance, it's been so long since I've seen you with your hair short! But it looks fine, doesn't it?" she asked, turning to his father.

"Yup," he said, "is that the regulation length?"

"No, they don't tell you what length your hair should be. I just felt I should get it cut, that's all. Well, would you like a tour?"

"Yes!" his mother exclaimed, trying to sound enthusiastic, but overdoing it in her nervousness. He showed them the admin building, the lodges, his bed, neatly made, with the pictures of the two of them and of Kathy on a horse, standing beside it. He showed them the dock where they went swimming, the road that they were leveling, the baseball diamond where he had gotten the winning hit.

His mother thought everything was lovely and tried to ask intelligent questions. But his father was non-committal, even less talkative than usual. "What do you think, Dad?" Keith said, at length.

"Oh," his father said, pursing his lips and nodding, "very nice. Very nice, indeed." Keith looked at him closely; "nice" wasn't a word his father regularly used. But his father, who would have been a great poker player when it came to concealing his reactions, revealed nothing.

He had saved the best for last. "This is our chapel," he said as they walked in, his voice betraying his pride. "Mr. Wilkerson preaches here on special weekends," he said, his voice unconsciously dropping to a whisper. His parents nodded appreciatively, taking in the stained pews and natural wood walls, the high-peaked ceiling, and hand-carved beams. "It's lovely!" his mother whispered, sensing how anxious Keith was for their approval. "Mmm," his father added dutifully.

They walked down a path and over a little covered bridge across a brook that flowed into the lake.

There was a bench nearby, overlooking the water, and the three of them sat down on it. There was a silence, as everybody waited for someone else to say something. Finally his mother faced it head on: "Keith, are you happy here?"

"Sure," he said, not wanting to get into it.

"Why?"

Keith hesitated before replying. Whenever his mother was upset about something, it was useless for her to make small talk and pretend that nothing was the matter. Until she got it all out and said what she had to say, she would be miserable behind her smiles and super-politeness. So he took a deep breath and started. "I don't know," he said thoughtfully, "life — at least my life — seems to be making more sense to me here. I guess I'm getting a new way of looking at things. And a new way of living, too."

"How?"

Keith shrugged. "God is real. That's really all there is to it. You start from there, and all the rest sort of falls into place."

"What falls into place?"

"Well, He made us. And He loves us. So much that when He saw us messing up our lives and the world and all, it really hurt Him, and He sent His Son to die for us, so that we don't have to stay the way we are and can be forgiven for all that we've done."

"But you learned all that in Sunday school when you were little," she said. "Why is it suddenly so important now?" His father said nothing, gazing at something down at the other end of the lake.

"It should have been important all along, I guess." Keith picked up a stone and flipped it into the lake. "Then maybe I wouldn't have run Mr. Henderson off the road." He looked up. "By the way, I want you to sell my motorcycle for me."

"But that's the thing you love more than anything in the world!" his mother said, startled.

Keith smiled. "That *was* the thing I loved more than anything in the world."

"Bob!" his mother said, turning to his father, exasperated, "are you hearing this?"

"Every word," his father said, not taking his eyes off the far end of the lake.

"Well for heaven's sake, say something!"

"What's to say? He's obviously marching to a different drummer."

"What does that mean?" she said, getting angry at him now.

"It means, Cynthia," he said, angry now himself, "that as far as he's concerned, our way of living — our friends, our goals, the things we've worked hard for and stood up for — is no longer of any importance to him."

"That's not true!" she exclaimed, and then hesitated. "Is it, Keith?"

Keith prayed to himself before answering. "*Keith*?" his mother insisted.

"Mom, I love you and Dad very much. I always will," he faltered when he saw the tears come to her eyes. "But my life is not my own, anymore. I've given it to the Lord. I belong to Him, now, and He is sort of rearranging my priorities. Like, when I finish at the Farm, I'd thought of maybe going to Bible school and becoming a missionary . . ." his voice trailed off as he saw his father shaking his head.

"This is exactly what I was afraid would happen!" his father declared. "They've brainwashed him, ruined him — "

"Nobody has brainwashed me, Dad," Keith said, beginning to get angry himself.

"Then who's giving you these ideas? That's what I'd like to know!"

"Bob!" his mother said, alarmed that the two of them were right back where they had been the night Keith left — on the verge of blows.

"At least he wants to go to college now —"

"You call *that* college?" he said, looking at her with disgust.

"Lord, this isn't going too well," murmured Keith with a smile, managing to regain his equilibrium, which infuriated his father even more.

"Look, Dad," he said calmly, "I'm sorry for getting angry. None of this is going to make any sense to you, unless and until you understand the basic motivator. If God *is* real, if He cares, then that changes everything, don't you see? It would be wrong to go on doing your own thing, instead of doing whatever is His thing for you. But until

153

you know He's real yourself, until you make the same connection — the Jesus connection, one of the guys called it — you're going to think that I've flipped, and that other people are telling me what to do, or what to think. And nothing I can possibly say or do in the meantime, will make any difference."

His father said nothing, and his mother began to weep silently. "Mom, don't," Keith said, taking her hand. "I shouldn't have tried to explain; it's not something you can get with your head. But your heart will sort it out sometime, if you'll let it. Just remember this: I've never been happier or felt more fulfilled in my life. And while I'm not sure yet what God will have me doing with my life, I know who I am, and I know that whatever it is, it will be just the right thing for me. In the meantime, I trust Him, and I really know what it means to have peace in my heart."

He paused and looked at her. "You can trust Him, too, Mom, even if you don't really know Him yet." And she smiled and patted his hand, to assure him that she would be all right.

Keith's visit was not the only one that was not going too well, that Sunday afternoon. Ray's girlfriend, Sal, was also visiting, and she was so shaken, she was almost speechless. Almost, but not quite. "You're thinking of *what*?"

"Keep your voice down!" Ray said, shushing her, and looking around furtively. They had walked behind the boathouse and then stepped back into the woods, where they couldn't be seen — or heard, as long as they spoke in modulated voices. Only Sal was in no mood for modulating.

"Would you mind saying that one more time?" she said, her eyes narrowing. "I cannot believe what my ears just heard!"

"I said, I was thinking of turning myself in for that bank job." He said lamely.

"Are you out of your *mind*? The papers said you got more than $30,000! That's what's waiting at the end of the rainbow for you and me, when you get done doing your time in this prison! And you want to boot that all away, and maybe get a half-dozen more years added on? What the hell has gotten into you?"

"I think maybe it's coming from the other direction, Sal," he said, hoping she would smile, but she only glared at him. "You remember that dream I had, about the mist coming all around me and healing me?" He waited, but she wouldn't even nod. "Well, a lot of things like that have been happening to me. I'll dream about something, and the next day in chapel, Mr. Wilkerson preaches about the same thing I just dreamed about. Or I'll say, without even thinking about it, 'Lord, I'm out of socks,' and a little later someone will come up who'd gotten my socks mixed in with his."

He looked at her, but there was no comprehension, and so he went on. "And what's happening to the other guys here is really something. I mean, they're actually turning into better people, before my very eyes. And man, I didn't think that was possible!"

"What have they got to do with you?" she asked pointedly, and from her tone it was clear that nothing he had said had made the least impression.

"Well, I feel like something in me wants to change, too. Those guys all made a commitment to God — that was the night I decided to split — and I have the crazy feeling that He's waiting for me to do the same thing, and hoping that I'll do it."

Sal looked at him in stunned unbelief. What page are you *on*, baby? You, Razor Daniels, getting religion? Oh, sugar, come off it!" and she started to laugh. "That's it, isn't it? You're putting me on," and she looked at him sidewise, the way they used to, when they were teasing one another. Only he wasn't smiling.

Her laughter died away. "You're serious, aren't you?" she said after a while. "You're really serious." Her voice was a little awed. He waited, not knowing what to say. "Well, where does that leave me?" she said, finally.

"I haven't thought it all through, Sal," he said lamely. "I guessed I thought — maybe we'd get married . . . You were always hinting around that that's what you'd like —"

"That was then; this is now!" she cut him off. "If you think for one minute I'm going to marry some no-fun holy Joe, you got another think coming! I mean, Sal's got some living to do!" and she put her hand on her hip. "And I'm going to do it, with or without you!"

She could see he was hurt, but she decided he needed a little punishing. "Wait till they hear on the street that Razor Daniels has gone chump! Why even Charlie the Chicken will spit on you!"

Ray grabbed her by the shoulder and swung her to him. "I haven't turned chump, baby," he said menacingly, and instantly her mood changed. Rubbing her body against him, she nuzzled his neck and purred, "Now that's more like it! There's my man," she said, and her hand started stroking his back.

For a moment, he returned her embrace, pressing her close. "My, my," she whispered, "three months must have been an awfully long time!" and she slipped her hand inside his shirt.

Ray pushed her away, though it was all he could do to bring himself to do so. "I'm sorry, Sal, I can't. Not now. Not this way — "

"What do you mean, not now?" she said, her eyes blazing. "Look at you! You want to so bad, you're trembling like a leaf!"

"I mean, you and I, the way we are together," he fumbled for the words, "it's got to be right — "

Finally, she fully understood. "You said you hadn't made any commitment like those other guys," she said, speaking slowly, "but I got news for you, buster: you just have." She turned and started walking out of the woods, rolling her hips. "Take a good look, Mr. Daniels," she called back over her shoulder, "because this is the last you're ever going to see of old Sal!"

He watched her go, until she was almost out of sight, then ran after her, calling, "Sal! Wait!"

But she didn't slow down until she reached the

157

car, a white Mercedes, with the top down. "Incidentally," she said, once she had gotten in, "I'm surprised you didn't ask about the car." And she smiled up at him, as she turned on the ignition. "I borrowed it from a friend," she said sweetly, biting off each word, as if were a piece of a candy bar, "a rich, white, fun friend!" and she threw the car in reverse and then roared out the driveway.

14

The Trip

"You know," Randy said, when I saw him a few days later, "there's nothing like a visit from home to really set things back."

"What do you mean?" I asked. I had just gotten back from a meeting with my brother in Texas, and had wondered how things were going.

"Well, Keith's parents came last weekend. From what Simon tells me, he handled it pretty well, all things considered. His mother came unglued, which is good, because at least she got her feelings out. But it's his father who's the problem." I raised my eyebrows, and Randy explained. "He refuses to see it, and he's blaming us for brainwashing his son. And his father's the one whose approval means so much to Keith."

"How's Keith doing now?"

"Not too good. He's started spacing out again. Simon has got the guys all speaking to him, when they catch him at it, but still . . . And yet, he's not the one I'm really worried about."

"Who is?"

"Ray," he said, shaking his head. "Don, he's gone as hard as a rock! He's like he was in the beginning, only now he doesn't bother fronting it. And nobody can reach him. He won't even talk about what happened with his girlfriend, when she was here. But you can almost hear the bitterness, burning its way like acid through his gut. Norman saw her leave. He said she must have been doing forty when she went through the main gate." He smiled. "I hate to think what she did to the suspension of that car on the frost heaves in that road out there!"

"It's what she did to the suspension of our friend Ray that matters," I smiled. I looked at the lake. "You know what I think? Maybe it's time for Alpha to take a canoe trip."

Randy slowly grinned and nodded. "A little stress to bring the pot to a boil. I'll suggest it to Simon, but of course the initiative will have to come from the group. It'll have to be their thing. Let's see," he paused to reckon, "there's nine of them, and Simon and me, and if they decide to go next weekend, that's Norman's weekend on — that's six canoes in all. Good! I'll try it out on Simon right away."

The camp's canoes were stored on their multiple trailer, down by the barn-shaped equipment building. Aluminum, their bottoms bore the scars of many white-water trips, for the staff had learned that stress situations — those in unfamiliar terrain and unpredictable circumstances which threw a person out of control — brought out the true nature of those involved. And nothing put one out of control

160

faster than trying to negotiate a tricky stretch of rapids.

The group took to the idea as Randy had anticipated, and that night they submitted their plans to Randy, for his approval and the benefit of his experience, for he had done extensive canoe-tripping. Simon joined him in going over the plans, and Norman took copious notes. It was decided that they would go down a river in the Adirondacks that Randy had done the year before, and they would make a three-day trip of it, which actually meant two full days on the water, when they got done with all the driving. They planned to start with lunch on Friday and go just far enough that first afternoon to tire the new men, without exhausting them, and then on the next afternoon, they would camp early, on the lake adjacent to the river, so that there would be some time for fishing.

"Too bad it's not Shekinah; Peter Rios is the fisherman in this camp, not me. But we'll see what we can do."

On Sunday morning, they would paddle across the lake and have lunch on the near end of the portage that would take them to the river. That way, they would save the best for last — two hours of white-water canoeing, before they reached the place where the van with the canoe trailer would be waiting for them. They would actually have to take two vans, to jockey them around so that there would be a ride waiting for them when they finished. And they would need them anyway, on account of all the equipment they were taking.

But as they worked out the logistics of which van would go where, with whom, it began to sound like a brain-teasing puzzle, and Norman, who was taking notes — and scratching them out and writing more — finally groaned and said, "I never knew a little canoe trip could be so complicated!"

"It's the planning ahead of time that makes it seem so easy," Randy replied and then laughed. "Now let's double-check their provisioning."

The trick was, of course, to wind up with nothing left over, except for emergency rations, because every pound of unused supplies was an extra pound that needed to be carried over the portages. So they planned two breakfasts, three lunches, and two suppers, for twelve very hungry people, not counting on the fish they would catch Saturday afternoon, because that was the sort of thing it was unwise to count on. The guys would be hungry enough to eat whatever they caught, along with their suppers.

"Okay," said Randy, "how will we divide up the canoes? Prayerfully," he said, answering his own question. "Keep in mind that we want the biggest guys in the stern, because they're the ones that will have to carry the canoes. And that means the three of us, too," he smiled.

"Ray and Keith and Stas," Simon said, simply. "But who's going in the bow of which canoe — that's a little harder."

"We need to take the smallest guys with us," Randy said. "Why don't I take Thomas, since he's newest, and Simon, you take Polo, and Carlos can go with you, Norman. Who does that leave?"

"Larry, Raul, and another new boy named Tony."

"How's Tony doing?"

"He's a little skittery, but he'll be all right."

"Okay, put him with Stas; he'll steady him down."

Norman raised his pencil from the notepad. "What about Larry? He's still a little flakey and not exactly what you'd call a fast learner."

"Put him with Keith," Simon said, after a moment. "He's good with Larry — remember the baseball game?"

"Okay, then that leaves Raul with Ray — good!"

"That leaves only the mosquito nets and ground and rain covers," Randy said. "We'll take three four-man set-ups, so each of us can be in one."

Simon shook his head. "Don't put Polo and Carlos in the same tent; they'll be up all night jawboning at one another."

"Okay, we'll switch Polo and Larry; Raul can keep Polo quiet." Randy stood up and stretched. "I think that's it. Don't forget to tell them to bring extra socks."

"Hey, Norman!" Simon said, clapping him on the back. "We're finished, man. You can stop pushing that pencil."

"I'm not pushing it," Norman explained. "I'm holding it together. It broke a couple of minutes ago, but you guys were talking so fast, I didn't get a chance to tell you."

Friday morning after breakfast, Randy backed one of the camp's vans up to the canoe trailer,

163

and Alpha group began the meticulous loading process. Food boxes were counted and numbered, and went in the back of the vans, with bedrolls of clothes and personal articles rolled inside of sleeping bags next, and the mosquito-netting and ground cloths last, because they were the most delicate.

It was a glorious day — the sun was out, and the temperature was in the mid 80's but there was a good steady breeze to keep it from getting too hot. "Man!" said Randy, hitting the steering wheel, "what a perfect day for a trip!"

"And the weather report says that it's going to hold like this all weekend," said Norman. "And did you see the way those guys were clowning around? I don't think they've ever been this excited about anything!"

"All except Ray," Randy noted. "I wonder if anything's going to get through to him?" Norman looked at the map in his lap, shaking his head. "At least Keith seems to be more with it."

Randy checked the rear-view mirror to make sure the van was with them, and then stepped it up to 55. A little over five hours later, they reached their starting point, and when all the canoes and supplies were off-loaded, Randy drove the van with the trailer over to the river, with Simon following in the other van, to bring him back. Near the river, just below the bottom of the rapids, he pulled into a gas station, where he had made arrangements to park their truck for two days. Getting out, he went in to talk to the owner, a grizzled old character who spent words as if they were silver dollars.

"Hi, Mr. Hackett, how are you today?" he said, grinning. He had talked to Mr. Hackett in previous years and knew what to expect.

"Good enough," was the reply.

"Beautiful weather for a canoe trip — how's the river?"

"High."

"Oh?" said Randy, raising his eyebrows. "From all that extra snow we had last winter?"

"Ayuh."

"But you said on the phone that others had been coming down the river."

"Ayuh." He nodded. "But they was mostly walking."

"You didn't tell me that," Randy said, frowning.

"You didn't ask me."

"Well," Randy said, as Simon came in, "where shall I leave the truck?"

"Out back."

And then Mr. Hackett came out with the longest speech Randy had yet heard him make: "That there river's higher than I've ever seen it, and I've been here thirty-seven years. You young fellahs be careful!"

Randy looked at Simon. "We will, Mr. Hackett. And thanks. See you Sunday."

"Ayuh."

As the sun approached its zenith, six aluminum canoes set out in single file across the lake. At least, they were supposed to be in single file, but it would take a supreme optimist to find anything approaching order in their formation. In the stern of the lead canoe, Randy was doing a competent J-stroke, pulling his paddle through the water, and then levering it sideways against the gunwale, to counter-act the effect of the stroke he had just completed. In synchronization with the strokes of Thomas, his bowman on the opposite side, he kept the canoe going smoothly and seemingly effortlessly in the direction he intended. And Norman in the fourth canoe, and Simon bringing up the rear, seemed to be doing reasonably well.

Not so, the others. Keith had done canoeing at camp and knew what to do, but it was a total, confusing mystery to Larry, whose solution was to go passive and drift along, going through the motions, but disengaged. And though Randy had patiently explained the J-stroke to the other two sternmen, and had them practice it under his supervision, and told bowmen and sternmen not to change sides just for the sake of changing, but to settle into a rhythm, the other three canoes were soon all over the lake. Bowmen and sternmen were yelling at one another and changing sides every two or three strokes, or both paddling on the same side which tended to send them in circles. As a result, Norman and Simon had to spend much of the afternoon playing sheepdog and herding the rest back into line.

Randy and Simon decided that they would knock off early that afternoon, and so they camped half-way down their second lake, instead of at its foot, as they had intended. Setting up the shelters was a continuation of the three-ring circus that the canoeing had been, and the chaos

166

that had reigned on their portage. It was a miracle that no one had put a hole in a canoe or dropped his bedroll into the lake.

Dinner was a disaster. Ray burned the hamburgers, Polo kicked over the pot of baked beans, Thomas and Carlos got into an argument about who was supposed to butter the rolls — and the staff, who could have put a stop to it, for some reason didn't. After supper, as they sat wearily and glumly around the fire, Randy spoke to them.

"You guys need to see why it went so badly today," and he left it to them to see what was wrong. It took a while, but it gradually developed that they had gotten completely into themselves and out of Christ, and some had not even bothered to pray, when Simon asked the Lord to bless the trip and protect them, when they started out. They were convicted that they had forgotten all about Jesus, and gone back to their old way of doing things, instead of His. They were sorry, and by the time they were ready for bed, there was a different attitude around the campfire.

And it carried over to the following morning. The mood of the camp was a little quieter, and a lot more peaceful. Breakfast was egg-in-the-hole — a piece of toast with a circle cut out of the center, and an egg fried on top of it — and bacon on the side. And breakfast was cooked just right. "Mmm," Simon said, "that's more like it! Whoever cooked this was in the Spirit!" Raul beamed, resisting the urge to say that he had.

Later, on the water, there was more

consideration for one another, and as a result, they covered the last half of the lake in about half the time that it took them to paddle the first half. On the portage, too, there was a difference. Now the bowmen stopped to make sure that the sternmen had their canoes balanced on their shoulders properly, before taking off down the trail themselves.

"All *right!*" said Randy appreciatively, when they had stopped for lunch, "this is the way it's supposed to be. There was a good spirit out there, this morning! Did you notice the difference?" And they all nodded. "The difference is Jesus," he said simply. "When you're paddling along, and you have nothing else to think about, keep your mind on Him. You'd be surprised the difference it makes."

By that afternoon, they were back on schedule, and still had enough time to set up camp a little early and do some fishing before dinner. There was a quiet, marshy inlet, with lily pads and water reeds in it, and Randy suggested that they drift over there, and try a few casts. "*Drift*," he repeated, for Polo's benefit, "*quietly.*" And so they did, the sternmen softly dipping their paddles into the water and pulling them through without a splash, the bowmen poised, ready to cast.

And before long, there was a tug on Thomas's line. "I got one, I got one," he whispered, and started reeling in as hard as he could.

"Jerk the line, and set the hook," whispered Randy in the stern, but it was too late. As suddenly as the line had gone taught, it went

168

slack. Thomas was crushed. "Don't worry," whispered Randy, "there's more in there." And Thomas perked up and tried again. There was a commotion in Simon's canoe. Carlos had caught a little bass that couldn't have been more than six inches, but he held it aloft, as proud as if it were a blue marlin. "Look, you guys!" he said in a loud stage whisper, and Randy covered his mouth to keep from laughing.

Polo was fit to be tied. Of all people to catch the first fish, his arch rival! "What is that, a minnow?" he shouted, "I wouldn't even bait a hook with that!" Simon took his paddle, and in one spraying swat, drenched his bowmen with water. "*Hey*!" yelled Polo, "what'd you do that for?"

"Because your blasted jealousy has just ruined the fishing here for the rest of us! Now shape up, or you're going to be swimming home!"

They paddled over to another area and drifted in again. This time, several of the guys caught fish, but the largest of the day, a beautiful small-mouth bass, was caught by Thomas. "Oh, wow!" was about all he could say, over and over, as they cleaned their catch. And when they fried them up in butter, Norman handling the pan so that nothing would go wrong, Thomas still couldn't believe it. "That's the biggest fish I ever caught!" he paused. "That's the *only* fish I ever caught!" Everyone laughed. "Oh, Mama, if you could only see your boy Thomas now!" And the camp roared with laughter.

The next morning dawned as bright and fair as the two previous days. It being Sunday, they had a prayer service before breakfast, taking turns praying as they were led. And as it turned out, almost all the prayers were prayers of thanks. Randy caught Simon's eye, and nodded, smiling. Simon nodded back.

They ate quickly that morning. Everyone was anxious to get to the river. The morning was hot and sultry, the breeze that had cooled them the past two days being absent. As they went across the last lake before the river, the sun beat down. Most of the guys had taken off their shirts and were wearing only the orange kapok life jackets which Teen Challenge required all of them to wear. No one talked. They all seemed to be drugged by the unbroken sun and the endless plash-pull-sweep-plash of their paddles.

When they finally reached the portage at the end of the lake, the guys were beginning to sag. "Okay," called Randy, after conferring with Simon, "take a swim break." It was amazing how quickly they revived, splashing around and cavorting in the water, their cumbersome life jackets left on the shore. The staff joined in, glad for a chance to cool off, but a few moments later, Norman nudged Simon and nodded towards the main group. Ray was standing waist deep, a little removed from the rest. As Norman and Simon watched, Raul waved to Ray for him to come on and join them, and when he wouldn't, Raul splashed him. Ray shouted a string of obscenities at him that cast a pall on the festivities, and Randy called everyone out.

When they had dried off, Randy called them together. "Was anyone offended by Ray's language?" Almost all of them nodded. "Then tell him." And they did. Ray glared at them; it was obvious that he was contemplating using some more. But he remained silent. "Now what in blazes is going on with you two, anyway?" Randy demanded. Neither one of them spoke. "Raul?"

"It just seems like I can't do anything, but that he's all over me!" Raul finally said. "Paddle harder, switch sides, don't switch sides, you're goofing off on the portages — it's been like that the whole trip!"

"Well, why didn't you say something?" Simon asked. "Why didn't you bring it into the light?" No answer.

"I think I know why you didn't," Randy said. "It's because you've gone back to your old thing of people-pleasing. You didn't want him not to like you, isn't that it?" Raul waited and then nodded. "Raul, don't lose what you've gained, man! Stick to pleasing Jesus. Look what your old way has gotten you. Are you happy?" He shook his head. "Is Ray pleased with you?" He shook his head more firmly. "Then start speaking what the Holy Spirit gives you to say, and if something isn't right, get help." Raul nodded.

"And as for you," Randy said to Ray. "If you've got a mad on about something, and you won't let anyone help you, then you can just sit in it, until you decide to do something about it. But don't make Raul, or anyone else, your scapegoat, understand?" Ray said and did nothing, then finally gave the slightest of nods.

As they began to get lunch ready, Simon pointed out a cloud on the southeastern horizon

to Randy, who promptly stuck his hand out at
arm's length and tried to cover the cloud with it.
"No bigger than a man's hand," he said, wryly.
But the wind had picked up again, and it was
coming from the southeast.

15

Out of Control

The river was a good three feet higher than Randy had ever seen it, and he stood a long time at the end of the portage, just looking at it. The water raced along, not foaming or babbling, but moving with an ominous force that he had not seen before. Already clouds were beginning to drift overhead. Simon, coming up behind Randy, looked up at the sky and said, "We may get a little wet before this afternoon is over."

"Yes," Randy agreed, only he was looking at the river.

"Do you think it's safe?" said Simon, picking up his concern.

Randy nodded. "If we're careful, we should have no problem. But we'd better forget about shooting any rapids this year. We'll portage around every one. Mr. Hackett was right when he said this would be a walking trip." When the others had reached the end of the portage, he called them around him. "The water is too high

173

to try any of the rapids today. I want everyone to stay exactly in line. I will be pulling in to shore well above each rapid, and I want you to start turning in to shore as soon as you see me begin to turn. Do *not* wait until you get down to where I turned. Is that understood?" and he checked every one of their faces, before continuing. "When you get to shore, you can let down along the shore-line, holding onto the bushes and so on, until you reach the place where I'll be waiting for you." Again he waited until he had visually checked their responses, and they all nodded assent. "Now I want everyone to have his lifejacket laced up all the way, and I don't care how hot it is." He paused. "And that means you, Ray," for Ray had left his open for comfort.

And so saying, he showed them how to load their canoes by the river-bank, the sternman holding the canoe, while the bowman got in position. "I want you sternmen to let your canoes down the side of the river, holding onto the bushes until every canoe is loaded and in the water. Don't cast off until you see me give the signal."

He looked up. "Oh, one more thing: if you lose anything in the river — bedroll, supply box, camera, I don't care what it is — let it go. Don't try to go after it. Is *that* understood?" And again they all nodded. "Okay, let's go," and he got in and let himself down the side of the river.

Soon, all six canoes were side by side, like fingers sticking out from the shore, or horses straining at the starting gate. Randy circled his arm over his head and pointed down river, and they let go. The river picked them up and

174

propelled them forward like little chips, so that their primary responsibility was guiding their canoes, not moving them. At first they were uptight, clutching their paddles and stroking more than was necessary. But after a while they began to relax, lulled into a false sense of peace, for the only indicator of their speed was how quickly the scenery on the sides of the river was passing by. And then, up ahead, they heard a roaring.

"Okay, now pay attention!" Randy called out, and as they swept around the next bend, he suddenly started pulling for the left-hand bank. Immediately, all the other canoes turned to the left also, and started letting themselves down to his canoe, even though they were well above him and could have come farther down without any trouble. "Good!" Randy said, when they were all ashore. "This portage isn't going to be easy, because it hasn't been used very often, although," he said, catching a glimpse of a fresh blaze cut in the trunk of a nearby tree, "it looks like it's been used in the past couple of weeks."

They portaged down through the woods beside the rapids. "They don't look too bad to me," Keith said to Randy, when they reached the foot of the rapids and were preparing to put back into the river. "I've done white-water canoeing in rapids tougher than those. You just shoot the V's and stay clear of the power waves."

Randy nodded. "You're right; those really aren't too bad. We probably could have shot them, if everyone knew what they were doing. But when things start going wrong out here, one mistake compounds into others so fast that —" he stopped himself. "It doesn't matter. We prayed about it, and I got a check in my spirit about doing any at all, and so we're not going to. Besides which, they get a lot tougher, further down."

Soon, they were back on the water, enjoying the feeling of being on an amusement park ride, where all they had to do was sit back and watch the scenery pass by. The only thing to spoil the afternoon was the clouds that now completely obscured the sun, and grew steadily darker.

Two more portages were executed without incident, and Randy called them together at the end of the latter one. "Okay, you guys have been doing good. I know you're disappointed about not being able to go down the rapids, but look at everything else we've got to be grateful for. It's not even raining!" And as he said that, several large drops splatted down on the rock where he stood. "Well," said Polo, "we can be grateful it isn't raining any harder than that!" and they all laughed.

"Now, listen," Randy called their attention back to what he was about to say. "White Birch Rapids are coming up. They're so bad, we portaged by them last year, even when the river was low. So stay alert." And they followed their now-familiar loading procedure, and waited for him to give the signal. "Ho-oh!" he called out like a wagon-master, and waved them underway.

Almost immediately, they flashed by the first large tributary that they had seen, and it too was swollen with run-off. Once they were past it, they noticed the difference in their speed, with all that extra water behind them. "Wow, we must be doing twenty miles an hour!" Polo called back to Simon, in the last canoe. "Well, fifteen anyway," replied Simon, "as fast as a man can run."

"Look at all them canoes in front of us!" Polo exclaimed. "They're really moving out! So are we! Hey, we look like a bunch of Indians on their way to attack somebody!" As they gazed down river, Simon called out, "I can see the white birch, way down there on the left, just before the bend. Won't be long before he turns in."

And in the lead canoe, Randy had also seen the white birch, and was looking for the portage clearing. As soon as he spied it, he shouted for Thomas to start pulling on his left side, and he switched to the right.

At that moment, Ray spotted five deer on the right bank and called Raul's attention to them. "Look at them dumb animals," Ray laughed. "They don't know enough to get in out of the rain," for by now it had started to pour.

"Hey, watch it!" Raul called back angrily, "you're letting us get broadside!" And he dug into the water on his right side to get them straightened out — and missed the fact that Randy had turned in. In the stern, Ray was turned around, his eyes fixed on the deer, who returned his gaze impassively. Over the gradually rising din of the approaching rapids, neither one of them could hear Randy shouting at them from shore.

In the third canoe, Keith was gliding along, his

eyes lazily on the stern of the canoe directly in front of him. "You know," he said to Larry in the bow, "this feels just like it used to, riding my bike, just drifting along, come rain or come shine." Larry couldn't hear him, but Keith didn't care. He smiled and licked at the rain that was sliding down his face. "Could use some goggles," he murmured, blinking, trying to keep the canoe ahead in sight.

Out of the corner of his eye, he caught something white, waving on the left bank. It was Randy. "Oh, my God!" he shouted, suddenly alert to what was happening. *"Larry, pull left!"* he yelled, but it was too late; they were around the bend.

In Ray's canoe, they knew what was happening, all right; they were about to be overwhelmed by it. They were in the grip of the river about to be swept into the first chute of water that funneled between two standing power waves like an inverted V. Ray screamed in terror in the back of the canoe, but Raul had enough sense to try to keep them pointed into the V.

They shot through the first V, and Raul caught a glimpse of one of the huge boulders under that water that caused the power wave. Before he could catch his breath, they were getting broadside again, and another power wave loomed directly in their path. "Go to the right!" Raul shouted and furiously pulled his paddle in towards the right side of the canoe, in sharp, digging strokes, intuitively doing the right thing. Even without any assistance from Ray, the canoe straightened and shot into the second V, for this was the one situation in which the bowman made the greater difference.

"We made it!" exulted Raul, without taking his eyes off the rapids in front of him. Down river, everything was a white cauldron of foam and flying spray and the noise was deafening. There was no time to think, only react. *"Right, right, right!"* he screamed and dug for all he was worth, for they were almost into the biggest power wave they had yet seen. But there was no response from the stern. Ray sat there, glassy-eyed, frozen with fear.

Even without him, they almost got by. But the stern swung into the power wave and crunched up onto the boulder beneath it. Like a whale blowing and then diving, the canoe began to upend. The right gunwale went down beneath the surface, water combed over the edge, and the canoe started to fill. *"Push off, push off!"* shrieked Raul, but it was too late. The canoe swamped, and in an instant they were up to their necks.

"Stay with the canoe!" hollered Raul, but Ray, galvanized now by the shock of being flung into the water, and seeing his bedroll with all his possessions in it bobbing away, crazily struck out after it. There were only two problems: he couldn't swim, and he had unlaced his lifejacket, so that now, instead of keeping his face out of water, it was up around his ears.

Meanwhile, Keith's canoe was now also inextricably caught in the rapids, with the first V fast approaching. "Jesus, Jesus, Jesus!" he yelled, and then, "Larry, pull right! Head us into

179

the V!" But his bowman, in mounting fear and confusion, had once again disengaged himself and gone totally passive.

Keith jammed his paddle in on the left side, and levered it hard against the gunwale, kicking the canoe straight. "Jesus help us now!" And the side of the canoe ground into the hidden boulder, but somehow scraped free. The sudden jolt, and the noise of the canoe tearing along the rock, did something to Larry who now started paddling furiously, only he was pulling them straight towards another power wave. "No, Larry, go right, *right*!"

Larry heard, and started pulling on the other side of the canoe. They hurtled through the second V, and Keith, instantly surveying the situation, shouted "Right again, go right!" and Larry dug on the right, as Keith pulled through on the left. Barely clearing the enormous power wave on their left, Keith spotted a flash of orange in the water up ahead, as they darted down the V. *"Pull left, Larry!"* he hollered, trying to make himself heard over the thundering rapids, and Larry shifted his paddle to the other side.

There, in the water ahead of him, was Raul, hanging on to the canoe for dear life. Seeing them coming, he waved and then pointed wildly, farther down the river. Sitting up as tall as he dared, Keith could just make out a distant life jacket bouncing along the surface. It was impossible to tell if there was a figure in it or not. He nodded at Raul as they flew past, and just straightened out to slip through the next V.

Where they logically should head now was to

the left, towards the outside curve of the river, where the water would be the deepest and the treacherous rocks would be the most covered. But the lifejacket, out of sight now, had been somewhere over to the right. "Pull right, Larry!" Keith decided, and they scraped through a narrow V and then another and then right over a whole series of smaller standing waves, their aluminum canoe whanging and groaning each time they slammed into another rock.

"Pray, Larry!" Keith shouted. "We just tore a hole and are taking on water!" and Larry prayed, and paddled harder than ever. They had the life jacket in sight again, and it looked like Ray was still in it, though one arm had come out of the armhole and his head was down inside of it. "Take him on our left side!" Keith shouted. "I'll try to grab him as we go by."

Larry pulled to the left, and in no time, they were on top of Ray, who bumped along the left side of the canoe. Flinging his paddle in the middle of the canoe where it would be out of the way, Keith leaned way over and managed to hook Ray under the arm. The canoe stopped, almost as if it had gotten hung up on a rock, and then started to broadside to the left. "Straighten us out, Larry!" and Larry tried, but it was no use; the drag in the stern was too great. In a second, they would be broadside, and at the mercy of a large power wave that was now approaching.

Keith looked down at Ray, whose face was out of the water now, but whose eyes were rolling around, unfocused. They were about to go over; he jumped out and held onto the side with one

181

arm, the other around Ray's chest. "Turn around," he hollered at Larry. "Kneel down, and steer for the V's!" And he steadied the canoe, as Larry got turned around. Suddenly the canoe was wrenched from his grasp, and in an instant, he was left alone with Ray.

Keith was a good swimmer; he had done competition swimming and skin-diving. And when he was in training, he could swim three laps underwater. But he had never experienced anything like the flying spray and gray-green turbulence he found himself in now. Slammed against rocks, powerless to direct where he was going, it was all he could do to stay concentrated on keeping Ray afloat. In the end, he gave up trying to keep his face above water at all times; it was impossible. Instead, he kept shoving him up to the surface every chance he got, remembering to get a breath himself occasionally as well.

He had one glance of where they were headed, down the V between two boulders so large that they stuck out of the water; in fact, this was more a waterfall than a V. He took a deep breath, grabbed tight hold of Ray, and felt himself plummeting downward. Driven well beneath the surface by the force of the fall, Keith lost hold of Ray.

Randy, the moment the three remaining canoes had made it safely to shore above the rapids, had raced down the portage, and had come out just below the last chute. When he got there, he peered through the teeming rain, but could see nothing but the water pouring out between those two high rocks. And then he heard it — a hollow, metallic *bang-bang-bang* — approaching. He looked up just in time to see a silver aluminum canoe fly through the chute, with Larry amidships, laughing his head off. *"Eee-yahhh!"* he cried, as the canoe launched out into the air, and he flung out his arms in a V for Victory sign.

Buwang! The canoe did a tremendous belly-slammer, but Larry had braced himself and now looked up, grinning. Spying Randy on the shore, he called out, "How was *that*, Mr. Larson?" and having lost his own paddle, he now grabbed Keith's and started making for shore, paddling first on on side, and then on the other, kayak-style.

Moments later there was another banging from above and in back of the chute, and now another canoe hove into sight — this one was riderless and got itself stuck sideways in the mouth of the chute, where it was pressed against the two standing rocks. And now Raul's face appeared above the canoe, and seeing them on the bank below, waved weakly to them. Then he started trying to free the canoe.

"Leave it there!" Randy called out to him, as loud as he could, trying to make himself understood above the furor of the chute. "Let go, and come down yourself!"

But if Raul heard him, he gave no sign. Finally, he did manage to work one end of the canoe free, and like a shot, it hurtled out of the chute, diving downward like a long torpedo, plunging beneath the surface below, and then re-surfacing like a playful porpoise. Seeing the empty canoe about to drift past them around the next bend, Larry launched his canoe back out into the river and rapidly stroked it on a collision trajectory. Randy hollered at the top of his lungs for him to come back, then just shook his head.

Larry banged into the empty canoe, just managing to get the nose of his own canoe on the downriver side. Working his way along the empty canoe, he got hold of it, found the painter in the bow, wrapped it around the nearest thwart, and started paddling both canoes to shore. He made it, landing considerably downriver from where Randy had been, and just held on to the bushes he found there, until help could come.

Raul, after he had freed the canoe, let himself go down the chute, and soon was dog-paddling for shore. By the time he reached it, Simon and Stas were with Randy, and all three were staring up at the chute. There was no sign of Keith or Ray.

16

Three up Front

"There they are!" Stas shouted, pointing to two orange forms that flashed through the chute and plummeted downward and out of sight again. Randy said nothing, but prayed harder than he ever had in his life. And the others began to pray, too.

Beneath the surface, Keith was more concerned about the whereabouts of Ray than he was of getting some air himself. His life jacket's buoyancy brought him to the surface, but why didn't Ray's? He was about to shed his life jacket and dive back under to look for him, when out of the corner of his eye, he caught a glimpse of orange. He reached down, was able to get a grip on Ray's arm, and jerked. Ray came free, leaving a shoe caught in the fork of a submerged tree limb, and Keith got an arm across his chest, and was able to support him on his hip. It was only then that it sank in that the water around him, though moving swiftly, was smooth.

He struck out for shore and was frustrated at

how weak he seemed to be; he couldn't make his body do what he wanted it to, and he was being swept downriver much faster than he was making lateral progress. But finally, he got close, and Randy, being anchored by Stas, reached a hand out to him. He grabbed it, and together they were able to get Ray ashore.

Now Randy took over. Laying Ray on his back, he lifted the back of his neck with one hand, and pulled his jaw forward with the other. Pinching his nose, he took a deep breath, and forced air into Ray's mouth. Then he repeated the process. After what seemed like an eternity, Ray's eyelids fluttered open, and he feebly pushed at Randy. "Wha' you doin'?" he mumbled, and then he started to be sick.

"He must have swallowed half the river," Keith said, suddenly exhausted, looking down at him. "Me, too," he added, and turned away to be sick himself.

By the time the rest of the party arrived, bringing their gear, he had somewhat recovered. But not Ray, who was sick as a dog.

Larry, on the other hand, was now jubilant. Talking faster and with more expression than anyone had ever heard him, he tried to describe his crowning moment. "Oh, man! You guys shoulda seen it! I came out of that chute like an airplane! Man, I was *flying!* Wasn't I, Mr. Larson? And before that, I came all the way down the rapids by myself — except in the beginning, when Keith was there to help me. But then, when he went over the side to get Ray, I was on my own. Man, was I scared! But Keith had

said to pray, and I was dong that, too, and —"
he stopped and looked at them. "Say, what's
the matter with you guys? What are you looking
at me that way for?" And then it dawned on
him, too, that he had said more in the last minute
than he had said at one time in the previous three
months — or three years, for that matter.

Simon grinned. "Well, don't stop talking on
our account. You just go right ahead and give her
the old play-by-play. What happened after Keith
left the canoe?"

"Well, I did what Keith said, and turned
around in the canoe and knelt down and — aw,
I'll tell you later." Then they all started
encouraging him, but he said, "No, I really will.
Don't worry; I think I'm going to have lots to talk
about from now on."

A low groan came from behind them. They
turned around to see Ray, propping himself up on
his elbow. "What happened to me?" he moaned.

"Well, if it isn't old Jonah," Randy said.
"What's the last thing you remember?"

"Well," he said, frowning and trying to collect
his thoughts. "There were some deer on the
bank, and it was raining, and then there was
somethng about — oh!" and he shuddered as the
scene came back to him.

"I'll fill in the blanks," said Raul,
matter-of-factly. "You panicked, and you froze.
You were as useless as — never mind; you sat in
the back of the canoe and watched, while I tried
to keep us headed straight. Then, when we
dumped, I yelled at you to hold on to the canoe,
but you went after your bedroll. And then along

comes Keith and Larry, and they go after you. I didn't see the rest."

Larry picked up the story. "We caught up with you about two-thirds of the way down. Your life jacket was unlaced, so it couldn't hold you up right, but it was still keeping you from sinking. When we grabbed you, that was about to capsize us, too. But rather than let go of you, Keith jumped out of the canoe, and got in the rapids with you, to hold you up, so you could breathe. That's the last I saw," and Stas put an arm around his shoulders, as he finished his second longest speech in three years.

"There's not much to add," Keith said. "Like the man said, I tried to keep your face above water when I had the chance."

"He saved your life," Randy said flatly. "When it could have cost him his own." He stopped to let that sink in. "When he pulled you in here, you weren't breathing. I didn't bother to take the time to see whether there was any pulse or not. I resuscitated you."

"It took a few minutes for you to come around," Keith observed.

Ray just looked at Keith. "Why'd you do it?" he finally asked.

"*Why?* What kind of a dumb question is that?" Norman exploded. "His brother was drowning. He didn't even *think* about why!"

"Well, thanks," Ray said to Keith.

"Is that all you've got to say?" Raul exclaimed. "I'd like to kick your teeth in!"

"No, leave him alone," said Keith. "He's got a lot to think about."

188

And with that, they went about gathering up all the gear, before it got any darker. When they finished, they were out one bedroll (Ray's), one food box, and one paddle (Raul's). It was nothing, compared to what the river could so easily have claimed and nearly did.

Driving home in the truck that night, Simon was fuming. "I can't get over Ray! Isn't *anything* going to get through to him? I mean, a man nearly dies, trying to save his life, and —"

Randy interrupted. "It got through to him."

"What makes you say that? I didn't see any —"

"I don't know; I just have a good feeling about Ray. I wouldn't be surprised if he didn't get much sleep tonight." He brightened. "Say, what about Larry, and Raul, and old Keith? Weren't they something?" And Simon enthusiastically agreed. "I wouldn't ever want to go through a scene like that again in my life, but brother, the Lord sure used it!"

When they got back to camp, it was well after dark, and the men were bone tired. It was all they could do to get the empty food boxes out of the van and onto their storage racks. And the younger, smaller fellows were so tired, the staff members carried their bedrolls up the hill for them. Not having one of his own, Ray took Thomas's. And then he stopped, and gathered up Raul's, too.

The second Sunday in October was set aside for a special occasion. Guests would be invited, and

189

parents of students in the program; Jose Martinez was instructed to pull out all the stops and make a lavish Sunday dinner, and they would have a commemorative service beforehand. Since Keith, Ray, and Raul would be leaving for the Farm the day after, Randy called Charles Russell, Teen Challenge's family counselor, to make a maximum effort to get their immediate relatives to come.

"Thought you'd want to know," Charles called him back. "Keith's mother and sister are coming, but his father's got some obligation he can't get out of. Seems he's going to Canada, camping with some business friends ..."

"Hmmm," said Randy. "What about Raul?"

"Well, by calling after ten at night, when his mother gets home from her factory shift, scrubbing floors, I was able to get her, too. She'd like to come, but she doesn't have a car. So I've arranged for her to ride up with Milton Delgado."

"Okay, good. And Ray?" There was a pause on the other end of the phone. "Randy, his girl told me off, like I've never been told off before. And there was somebody else with her in the background. They were laughing about it," he said, disgustedly. "But did you know he had a mother?"

"Yeah, he doesn't like to talk about her. I think he's ashamed — not of her, of himself."

"Well, that may be, but she was thrilled to hear what was happening. She hadn't heard anything from him for almost five months. When I told her about the program, she started praising God, she was so grateful. Sounded like she'd been praying for something like this to happen to him for years!"

"The household of the faithful shall be redeemed," Randy murmured.

"What?"

"Oh, nothing. How is Mrs. Daniels going to get up here?"

"She's going to try and get off work, and if she can, she'll come with Milton, too."

"Good job, Russ. I'm not going to tell any of these three about this. Let it be a surprise."

Saturday afternoon, there was a knock on the door of Randy's office. It was Ray. "Mr. Beteta sent me to see you," he said, his voice shaking. Randy told him to sit down and asked him what it was.

"I can't go to the Farm, Monday."

"But why not, Ray? The rest of Alpha thinks you're ready to go, and so does the staff. Ever since the river, you've been coming around more and more. I think you really want to live for the Lord now, even if you don't talk about it."

"That's just it," Ray said, his voice barely audible. "I do want to live for Him, now. Which is why I can't go on living a lie."

"What do you mean?" Randy said quietly, rocking back in his chair.

"I mean that the day before I first came to Teen Challenge, I held up a bank."

"You did *what*?" Randy's chair came forward.

191

"I held up a bank. You remember reading about 'the black hat bandit?' "

Randy frowned. "I vaguely remember something about it," he said.

"Well, that was me," said Ray. "I never told anybody, and the reason I came to Teen Challenge was because I was in violation of parole, and my P.O. was checking out my girlfriend's place, and I had no money with me and needed a place to hide out." Ray smiled at the recollection of what happened next. "Just about that time, I ran into one of your street workers, Mr. Delgado. He was so sincere; he told me that God had a new life waiting for me, if only I would go to Teen Challenge. So, I thought, why not? I needed a place, and suddenly this opens up right in front of me."

He laughed ruefully. "You know something, Mr. Larson? That Milton Delgado was right: coming to Teen Challenge has given me a new life. Only not the way he — or I — ever expected."

Randy was nonplussed. "Well, what happens now?" he managed. He had an idea, but he wanted it to come from Ray. "Well, I turn myself in, give back the money, and serve my sentence. I'll probably get at least four-to-six, since it's my second offense. Then, when I get out, I want to come back and complete the program."

"You may not have to wait that long, Ray. You're one of our guys now, and we'll go to court with you, just the way we went with Raul. I know it seems impossible, but I've seen God do some awfully big miracles in court. In fact —" Randy paused. For a moment, it almost seemed to him as if there might even be tears in Ray's eyes.

On Sunday morning, we had a large congregation in the chapel; just about every pew was filled. As we sang some of our favorite choruses, I glanced out over the faces. There were a lot of new ones: Polo and Larry and Stas and the others had already gone on to the Farm. But sitting in the first row were three familiar faces — Ray, Keith and Raul. I grinned at the thought of the Holy Spirit's push, and then recalled that morning four months before, when they had first come into 444. So much had happened ... Looking over the congregation, I tried to spot Mrs. Daniels. That would be her in the fourth row, beaming, sitting alongside of a Puerto Rican lady — who, of course, would be Mrs. Castenada, since Randy had said they were coming up with Milton. And towards the back, the lady in the suede suit and silk scarf, with the blonde girl in a pony-tail beside her — that would be Keith's mother and sister. I looked back down at the three up front; they had come in early, and so far, none of them knew that their relatives were here. They were in for quite a surprise.

Usually, when some of the men are about to leave for the Farm, we ask them to stand up and say a few words, and so when that time came, I said, "Tomorrow, three of our students are graduating, and two of them are going on to the Farm. I'd like all three to come up here and share with you what their time at Camp Champion has meant."

The three of them stood up, came forward, and turned to face the congregation. Almost immediately, Keith saw his mother and sister, as Kathy waved. And Raul soon saw his mother, too. He grinned and pointed her out to Ray, who looked — and then opened his mouth in unbelief. There was *his* mother, too!

"Well?" I said, turning to them, "who's first?" They all seemed perfectly willing to defer to each other, but finally Raul spoke up. "When I first came to Teen Challenge, I was glad enough to be here, because it beat sitting in jail for a bunch of years. But that was all; it didn't mean any more than that. *Life* didn't mean much more to me than sniffing glue and trying to hang around with guys I thought were cool. And then I found out that there was a little more to life than that — a whole lot more, in fact. I found out that there was Jesus. I found out that I didn't have to be cool any more, or care about what people thought of me. Because He's the only one whose opinion counts. I don't know what it's going to be like at the Farm, but I know that Jesus will be there, too. Because He's here. So I'm not going to sweat it."

It was Keith's turn. "I don't have much more to say than what Raul has just said. And by the way," he added, smiling, "when we first roomed together back in Brooklyn, he would have split before saying one-tenth that much to a crowd one-tenth this size." There was a ripple of laughter. "And I would have been right behind

194

him!" More laughter. "Me, too!" agreed Ray, and everyone laughed.

"I was a drifter," Keith resumed, when the laughter had died away. "I wasn't into pot or snow, but I was tripping out, just the same. I did it on my motorbike, and on booze when I wasn't riding. And sometimes when I was. Which was how I almost killed a man. I was checking out, as the guys put it, because I didn't like reality. And because reality was where I was forced to live, I spent as much time as possible out of reality. But no matter how far I took off and flew, I always had to touch down again. And there was old reality, waiting at the end of the runway.

"But I've discovered something that's very important, in case any of you are escape artists, too: there's only one way to cope with reality, and that's by walking through it, hand in hand with Jesus Christ. He's the Master of reality, just as the other fellow is the master of unreality and fantasy. I've taken Jesus's hand, and I'm not going to let go."

And now it was Ray who spoke. "The reason I'm not going to the Farm tomorrow, is because I'm going to jail, instead. You see, I held up a bank before I came here, and didn't tell anyone about it. I wasn't going to tell anyone about it, either. But then, the same Jesus that got to these guys began to get to me, too. Only I held out a little longer. You see, I was a hard guy — my street name was Razor, and I did my best to live up to it. But then one day, we went on a canoe trip. And because I was busy sight-seeing, instead of paying attention, I nearly got four of us killed.

In fact, I was more dead than alive myself, when this guy, standing next to me, jumped into the rapids to save me. Can you imagine that? A rich white boy risking his own life to save me!"

He paused, and no one breathed. "What you don't know is, all my life I've hated rich, white folks. If one of them had been dying in the gutter, I would have crossed to the other side of the street to avoid getting near him. My mother's here this morning, and she knows that's true." He nodded at her, and his mother nodded back, dabbing her eyes.

"Now I know what got into that white boy. And Raul, too. Because I was there the night it happened. Jesus got into them. But He didn't get into me. Not then. I ran away. And nearly got killed in the process.

"Well, I'm not running any more. I've got Jesus in me now, too, and that's why I'm going back to give myself up. You guys will be long through the Farm, by the time I get there," he said, turning to Keith and Raul. "But I'll catch up with you somewhere along the way."

And as he finished, I had the strongest feeling in my spirit that he would.

Epilogue

"You really don't need to hear a sermon after those testimonies," I said, standing up. "But I just want to add one thing to what they've said. The program isn't Teen Challenge; the program is Jesus. When these men leave here tomorrow, they won't be dependent upon this place, any more than Raul or Keith will be when they leave the Farm, eight months from now. Because they'll be taking the program with them. Jesus will be within them, only a prayer away, whenever they need Him.

"We have a saying around here: 'Wherever you go, there you are.' Because when the pressure gets a little heavy, there's a strong temptation to split, to escape. 'Maybe my life will be better on the other side of the country; maybe a change of environment is all I really need.' And those of you who are living in the world, you have the same temptations, I'm sure. 'If only I had a new job, a new family situation, a new church ...' Here we call it 'taking the geographical cure'. But it never works. Because wherever you go, there *you* are. *You* are the problem."

I glanced out the window at the trees and back again. "But the converse is also true: if you have Jesus, and are letting Him show you who you really are, and if you are cooperating with the Holy Spirit, as He goes about changing you, then you don't need to go anywhere. Because the circumstances right where you are, are the ones that God will work through. And if He should move you, like He'll be moving these three tomorrow morning, you won't have a thing to worry about, because wherever you go, there Jesus is."

I looked at the three of them. "And now I'd like to close with a prayer for these three young men. Lord, you tell us in the thirtieth Psalm, 'Weeping may endure for a night, but joy cometh in the morning.' We rejoice for these three, that they have entered into the joy of the morning. We pray that you will strengthen them, Lord, for whatever may await them. Gird them up and sustain them, and may they never stray from your side. Amen."

Monday morning — I would be leaving for Brooklyn in a few minutes, and Ray would be riding down with me. In the meantime, I stood on the porch of the admin building with Randy, watching the departure of the vehicle that would be taking Raul and Keith to the Farm. They waved goodbye, excited to be on their way, and I felt the slightest sadness come over me. Randy may have sensed it. "We've got three more coming in this morning — a former poly-drug user, a former child molester, and a former teenage alcoholic ... And here comes Ray, with that old beat-up suitcase of his."

"Right!" I smiled and picked up my briefcase. "See you Thursday," I said, and went down to the car.

The proceeds from the sale of this book will be used to build an additional home for young men like those whom you have just read about. If you would care to help Teen Challenge in its work, please consult your local phone directory, for the Teen Challenge Center nearest you, or write to:

Teen Challenge
444 Clinton Avenue
Brooklyn, New York 11238

Like his brother David, **Don Wilkerson**
was called to the ghetto street ministry
that was to become Teen Challenge,
which now has more than fifty centers in
urban areas throughout the country,
reaching out to drug addicts, alcoholics
and emotionally disturbed young men
from all walks of life. He has become a
nationally recognized authority on the
treatment of these problems, and has
written several books in his own right,
including one on teenage drinking to be
published this fall. Mr. Wilkerson lives
with his family at Camp Champion, and
divides his time between there and the
original Brooklyn Teen Challenge Center
of which he is director.

David Manuel is the author of *The
Jesus Factor, Like A Mighty River,* and
The Light and the Glory, co-authored by
Peter Marshall. Mr. Manuel and his
family live on Cape Cod, where they are
members of the Community of Jesus.